Copyright ©2023 Angel Leigh McCoy

What is Wyrdwood?
https://www.angelmccoy.com/wyrdwood-home/

DEDICATION

WRITING CAN BE A LONELY ENDEAVOR. Fortunately, I've been blessed with a remarkable group of peers who keep me steadfastly on task and who propel me toward my dreams.

The members of the Wily Writers writing group have been my guiding stars. We are a band of dedicated author-preneurs, actively publishing, who share information and encouragement.

Every weekday, we gather on Zoom for up to four hours. While we each craft our own stories, working in parallel, our spirits are intertwined.

We share the business and craft lessons we've learned, and when overwhelm, burnout, or imposter syndrome threatens to drown someone's creativity, we talk each other off the ledge. Best of all, we celebrate each other's successes as if they were our own.

I dedicate this book to the core members of this fellowship: Marsha Defilippo, E.S. Magill, Yvonne Navarro, and Loren Rhoads. You are my dear friends, my mentors, and my idols. Your generous dedication to supporting me makes you as responsible for the completion of this book as I am. Without your unwavering friendship, I might have surrendered to inertia long ago. My sincerest love and gratitude to you all!

ALSO FROM WYRDWOOD
by Angel Leigh McCoy

Cupid Missions series
Christmas Cupid

Catsitter Mysteries series
Catsitter's Conundrum
Catsitter's Curse
Catsitter's Collar (coming 2024)

Reluctant Undertaker series
Satyr (coming 2024)

Wyrdwood Welcome Trilogy
Stalking the Moon
Jumping the Moon
Hexing the Moon

Wyrdwood Historical Society series
Nurse Magdaleine
Charlie Darwin, or the Trine of 1809

Wyrdwood Origin Stories
Pipsqueak

♦

From Wyrdwood: Catsitter Mysteries #2

Catsitter's Curse

Angel Leigh McCoy

♦

Table of Chapters

INTRODUCTION

MAYOR BAGLEY *documents events.*

[BEGIN INCIDENT REPORT.]

In all my time as mayor of Wyrdwood, never have we come so close to disaster as in recent weeks. The giant under the mountain stirred. I admit, it terrified me. I'm not sure we have the magick it would take to fix things if he woke up all the way.

Some folks blame global warming, and they're partially correct. The titans won't slumber much longer if we keep tipping Earth off balance. What people don't realize is that Mother Nature has an army, and she will defend herself.

I questioned Kitty and Diana Kats again. Trouble finds them. I suspect King Muse bears some responsibility for that. He's a trouble*maker*.

These are their renditions of the story, given under the influence of a Bareface charm.

—Filed with the Wyrdwood Mayor's Office, Violet Bagley

You're off to great places! Today is your day!
Your mountain is waiting,
So get on your way!
— Dr. Seuss, *Oh, The Places You'll Go*

◆

CHAPTER 1

DIANA KATS *gets hung up.*

"Eagle Crenshaw, you better not leave me here!" I did not like the screech of panic in my voice. "I'm too young to die!"

Eagle disappeared from view. "Hang on." His footsteps moved away, becoming inaudible.

Unfortunate choice of words: hang on. I was *literally* hanging by the seat of my pants. My cohort in crime-busting, Eagle, had crawled through the cave's tunnel ahead of me on his belly, like a soldier, like a pro, and had emerged into the larger cavern beyond.

Being smaller and more stubborn, I refused to get down on my stomach. No way I was going to ruin my new jean jacket.

I figured I could make it through on hands and knees.

I'd been wrong. Amateur move.

The waistband of my jeans had gotten stuck on something, and no amount of writhing had freed me.

My nerves jangled. Stupid. Stupid! If I died there, my mom would kill me.

I had no business going underground with Eagle. Who was he, really? I'd only known the man for a week. He'd approached me at my workplace to see if I would help him with a case. Eagle's a private detective. A Normal who can't see magick. He lost his previous partner who had the spark. I don't mean the partner died. He just left.

So, because this is Wyrdwood and you can't spit without hitting the descendent of a god, mythic hero, or monster, he needed someone to guide him. He chose me, for some reason I have yet to understand. I do see beyond the veil. Both my parents descend from kith—magickal family lines. My mother comes from the dakini spirits of Tibet, and my father came from a long line of sphynxes. My blood is watered down, but I can still see sparky people and things. In other words, I see kith in their true form if they're not actively camouflaging themselves to appear Normal.

A kith's true form expresses their magickal DNA. Depending on how blue your blood is—or green or black or lavender—your true form shows it. We're almost all hybrids and mutts, of course. We've been interbreeding for generations.

The world at large—the Normals—can't know about us. They've proven—ad nauseum—that they will massacre every last one of us. Is it jealousy? Fear? Yes and yes. The end result is that they will exterminate our asses if they find out we exist. Fortunately, we have magick. And we have Wyrdwood.

Wyrdwood is one of a dozen shelter towns in the world. Magick in the area keeps us hidden from Normals, so we don't have to expend our own energy to keep up a veil. There are beings here in Wyrdwood—ancient beings—who fuel the magick that hides us.

Honestly, I don't know how kith in unprotected places do it. It's exhausting always having to pretend to be something you're not. In Wyrdwood, we live safely side-by-side with Normals. Heck, we have tourism. It's a beautiful place for a vacation. Kind of like Disneyland, except the characters walking around are normal on the outside and cartoons on the inside.

Some Normals know about us. Eagle is one of those. He can't see us, but he knows we exist. He believes in magick. There are humans like this. Maybe a loved one showed them, or maybe they discovered it on their own. For Eagle, it was his ex-partner who brought him into the fold. Before you enlighten a Normal, you have to ask permission from the mayor. I assume they did that.

Someone—Eagle wouldn't say who—had hired him to get pictures of an illegal mining operation. He took me with him because, "No one should ever spelunk alone." I was beginning to understand why.

Spying on gold miners had turned out to be less fun than Eagle had promised. What made me think I could stop a cabal of criminals who were doing who-knew-what-damage to the environment?

When Eagle first asked me to help him, I was skeptical. I was still skeptical while hanging by the seat of my pants in a cold, damp cave and watching him walk away from me. What if he'd been grooming me so he could get me away from civilization and hold me prisoner? What if...

I reined in my imagination with one word. "Stop." Of course, he was neither a murderer, nor a pervert, nor a psychopath. I may not have known him for long, but I'd spent more time sitting in his car with him than I'd spent with my own mother since moving back into her house.

He'd be back. As long as he didn't get stuck somewhere, too.

What if we both die? What if the ceiling collapses on us? What if...

"Stop."

I wasn't taking any chances. I wiggled and tugged. I grunted and growled. I kicked and clawed. I lashed and thrashed. I even farted. Nothing helped. I was stuck.

Exhausted, I collapsed, though my butt stayed held up by whatever had snagged my jeans. I rested my forehead on my arm and closed my eyes.

The rock walls, ceiling, and floor were closing in on me. In my head, I was having my own Death Star trash compactor moment.

I had my phone, but we'd already established there was no signal inside all that stone. I couldn't even call for help. At least I had a flashlight in hand. He hadn't left me in complete darkness. I had no choice but to wait.

Eagle and I had very different definitions of "right back."

I thought about my new job at the Sheriff's Department.

I was a computer engineer, not law enforcement. Last thing I wanted to do was confront—much less touch—criminals or guns. Instead, I dealt with email accounts, databases, and internet connectivity. They were my jam.

The job was going well. I learned long ago that it's best to under-promise and over-deliver. I'd established a routine and systems to make my work more efficient. They paid me for a full eight hours, though I really only worked about four—because I was just that good.

I spent a lot of work-time browsing the Internet. Most days, I cruised websites, researching for my mom. She was internet-clumsy, and she needed me. It surprised me how much that made me happy. My dad's passing threw her out of her element. She went from being a housewife-diva who wore high heels when she vacuumed to being a one-woman-band lugging all the instruments around on her back. Her life had become a cacophony because she had never learned how to play the harmonica.

Suffice it to say that the gaps in her knowledge of the practical world became glaringly and painfully obvious. My dad had handled everything except the housekeeping.

I, on the other hand, was lucky *my* husband was a loser, so I learned quickly how to take care of myself, the bills, and the repairs. When the po-po threw him in jail for running a Ponzi scheme, I moved in with Mom. I had no choice. They froze all our assets.

So, I help Mom as much as she'll let me. Funny that. The daughter teaches the mother how to manage grown-up responsibilities. I just wish she wasn't so stubborn about it.

I am well aware of the contradiction between my day job and the fact that I was moonlighting as the sidekick to a local private detective. It helped, of course, that Eagle was easy on the eyes. We had a vibe going that felt awesome. Being his sidekick made me feel alive, adventurous, and important. We spent most of our time stalking—I mean 'surveilling'—people. That meant sitting around in his car, at restaurants or bars, or even on foot. He took photos. He provided the snacks, and I provided the witty banter. It was a win-win.

I was having fun—or, at least, I had been until the cave.

So there I was, hung up in an underground tunnel, waiting for Eagle to—hopefully—come back. The weight of all that rock and dirt above me pressed down—not literally, but mentally.

My life flashed before my eyes...and then something moved against my leg.

I jerked. "Oh, hell no. Hell, no!" I arched up as high as I could go and stuck my arm down under me to where I could undo the top button and a few inches of zipper. Then I scrambled forward as fast as I could.

I left my pants and boots behind.

The cavern's floor was lower than the tunnel opening, so I dropped down head-first and hand-walked forward until I was all out. I stood up.

Eagle was back.

"I made it." I took a dignified stance, sniffed, and straightened my underwear.

"I see that."

Too much silence followed that exchange, and I was acutely aware that I was half naked. I took some comfort in the fact that my socks covered my ankles.

Eagle averted his eyes. "The miners are down that-a way." He indicated 'that-a-way' with a jerk of his head.

I could just make out the sound of running water punctuated by the low rumble of voices. "I hear them." I kept my voice low.

Eagle whispered too. "It's all open space from here on out."

"Better be."

More silence.

Then Eagle undid his belt. He opened the top button on his pants.

An uneasy trepidation filled me. "What are you doing?"

"You can have mine."

His jeans? Oh hell no, again. My phone was still in *my* jeans. I dove headfirst back into the tunnel, shining my light around and hissing to scare away whatever had touched me. My flashlight caught a pair of red glowing eyes that blinked at me before the monster turned and ran away. No idea what it was.

"Git!" I encouraged it to flee.

I had to scooch in all the way to my knees, but I managed to grab my jeans. Without me in them, they were a cinch to shake down and pull out. My boots caught inside the pant-legs and came along. I backed out of the tunnel, saying a prayer of gratitude that I hadn't worn my thong.

When I emerged, Eagle dropped his gaze.

I inspected my pants. Phone in pocket. No creepy crawlies, centipedes, snakes, rats, bats, or goblins. I put them back on. "I guess this is my home now."

"What do you mean?"

"No way I'm going back through that tunnel. You'll have to bring me food and water. It's your fault I'm here." I buttoned and zipped the jeans. "I'll need a sun lamp." The space was vast and had a somewhat-flat floor. "A bed and TV. Mimi, my dog. Oh, and you'll have to run electricity, plumbing, and a fiber-optic cable."

"Anything else, your highness?"

"I'm decent. You can look now." We both knew he'd already gotten an eyeful—not that I cared. I wore less at the beach. We all have bodies, after all. At least, that's what I told myself while I ignored my fading blush.

Eagle faced me. "I could knock you out and drag you through."

I widened my eyes as much as possible. "Okay, put your inner caveman away, Oog."

That earned me a crooked smile. "Well," he said, "if I have to bring you food, there'll be no more of that crap you eat."

I held up both hands, palm up, and shook my left one. "Panic attack I'll have halfway through that tunnel." I shook my right hand. "Versus never having ice cream again. Okay, you win. Just don't hit me hard enough to leave a permanent mark."

Eagle chuckled.

I inspected my boots for invaders then put them back on.

Eagle headed toward the opposite wall, taking his circle of light with him. "Stay quiet. These guys aren't foolin' around.

They have guns, and they'll use them."

I nodded, aware of how much noise my footsteps were making. I whispered, "And in here, no one would ever find our bodies."

◆ ◆ ◆

CHAPTER 2

KITTY *remembers the Fishgivens.*

For the record, my name is Kitty Kats. While my daughter Diana was adventuring with her friend Eagle, I was catsitting for Martha Fishgiven. Her husband Harold had just died, and she was staying with her sister while waiting for the coroner to release his body. She couldn't take the cats with her.

Martha would be gone for a few weeks. She intended to take Harold to England for burial in the family mausoleum. I'd agreed to catsit out of friendship and a sense of duty. Martha had been there for me when I'd had uterine cancer.

It had been fifteen years since I got the diagnosis. Diana was too young to be useful. Bob was too emotional. I'd been ready to go through the treatments and surgery on my own, but then Martha showed up. She, more than my other friends, supported me through treatment and a hysterectomy. I was alive and cancer-free because she had kept me from succumbing to negativity.

Martha was a godsend. How could I say no to watching her cats for her?

After a bit of jiggling, I got the front door open. My old friends' once-lovely home was a wreck. A tornado had spun through. Someone had pulled all the drawers out and strewn their contents everywhere. They'd skewed every picture on every wall and had tossed the linens off the mattresses. Heck, they'd tossed the mattresses off their bed frames.

I picked my way through the debris, tidying bits here and there. Martha had done nothing to clean up the mess. I couldn't blame her. In the best of situations, sorting through a deceased loved one's belongings was traumatic. I knew this from personal experience. I was still going through my Bob's things six months after his death.

But this wasn't just messy. It was torn up to a shocking degree. Who would do such a thing? Martha? Had she gone into a fit of grief and upended the house? That didn't seem like her. No. It more closely resembled what the police had left behind when they raided my daughter's house, searching for evidence to convict her husband—Kyle—of fraud. He'd perpetuated a Ponzi scheme on a bunch of vulnerable seniors, including my own Bob. It still made me see red, and my feelings of betrayal were nothing compared to what my daughter Diana felt.

I went to the master bedroom. Harold Fishgiven had spent his final weeks bedridden there. They had moved out the king-size bed and brought in a hydraulic hospital-style bed.

On the bedside table, I spotted a book I recognized.

"Oh, Harold." I picked up *The Cave of the Ancients* by T. Lobsang Rampa, the story of a Tibetan monk learning about the magickal nature of the universe. I had gifted him that book, many years earlier, on his birthday, with the inscription, "See you in the astral plane, my friend." Whenever he reread it, he'd made a point of telling me he'd learned yet another something new from it. It was our thing, his and mine. Neither his wife Martha nor my husband Bob had understood.

The fact that he'd been reading it right before being murdered made my heart ache. I hope his next life ends better.

The Fishgivens were full-time residents on Lake Talyllyn. Harold inherited the lakeside property and house from his parents. He grew up there.

Every summer, my husband Bob and I took our daughter to the campground on the lake. Our families became friends when Diana was just a toddler. The Fishgivens never had children, so they semi-adopted Diana as theirs to spoil. To Diana, they were Uncle Harold and Aunt Martha.

I always suspected that Diana was the real reason they invited us to their barbecues. She was much cuter back then.

The Fourth of July parties became a tradition for both our families. The Fishgivens threw a huge shindig with food, games, sparklers, and fireworks on the lake.

Of course, it's been at least ten years since my family vacationed there. Diana grew up and went to college. Without a kid to entertain, Bob and I didn't have enough energy to pack the camping equipment—not for just us two. Truth be told, we didn't have enough energy for much of anything. We were pitiful empty-nesters.

Bob worked right up to the end. I was a homemaker. In the evenings, we watched TV in our matching recliners. That was our life. It still would be, if Bob hadn't died.

There's nothing sadder than a barren recliner. Earning money wasn't the only reason I started catsitting. I needed to save myself from that recliner.

So many memories at the Fishgiven home—all of them sweet.

Bob and I are digging through a pile of coats in the master bedroom. We're both drunk on Martha's eggnog. Bob picks up a coat with a fur-lined hood and drapes it around his head. He looks like an Eskimo, and when he comes over and rubs his nose on mine, he says, "I love you, my darling seal." We laugh so hard, we fall onto the bed and end up snuggling there in a boozy cloud of other people's coats and colognes.

Whenever you enter the Fishgiven house, you find yourself in the room we jokingly called the 'ballroom.' Activity at Martha and Harold's parties centered in the vast room. It occupied a full third of the floor plan. All the other rooms opened off that central cavernous space.

A round table stood at the center of the ballroom. Someone had knocked a vase off it. Broken glass lay scattered across the marble tile floor. I couldn't have kitties stepping on broken glass. Not on my watch. I realized I'd have to clean the whole place up. After an initial flash of irritation, I calmed down and decided I didn't mind. It was the least I could do for my grieving friend.

The broom and dustpan were in a coat closet near the front door. I retrieved them and swept the shards into a neat pile.

The first time we go to the Fishgiven's, Harold answers the door with his signature line, "Hey! How the hell are ya? C'mon in!" Bob and I are both nervous. We don't know anyone there except the Fishgivens, but Harold shakes Bob's hand and hugs me. From then on, we're treated like family.

An alarm blared, loud enough to make me cringe. My first thought was 'Fire.' My second was, 'Not again!'

My life had sucked in recent weeks. When two of your neighbors' houses burn down, one right on top of you, you might just think you're cursed. I sure did.

It was the front door alarm. When I checked, I saw that the front door was ajar. I maybe didn't shut it all the way? The wind could've blown it open, triggering the alarm. I pushed the door closed and tugged to make sure it was secure, then I found the code Martha had texted me and silenced the alarm.

That was when I heard the "shuffle." Not like a card deck but like someone speed-walking while trying to keep from peeing their pants. It came from the living room.

I assumed—should've known better—that it was Martha's cats. The alarm must have freaked the poor babies out.

"Smaug? Faffy? Is that you, honies? It's okay. You're safe. Come and see me. It's your mom's friend Kitty."

Martha's kitties are a pair of tiny old ladies that I'd known since they were kittens. I saw myself as their auntie.

Behind me, the front door opened.

I twisted around to see who it was.

A person stood silhouetted against the bright exterior. Not a tall, broad, evil silhouette as I'd feared, but a small—smaller than me—bushy-haired silhouette.

"Holy jibeezus, Martha! I almost wet myself!" I lowered my weapon—the broom.

Martha laughed. "Happens to me several times a day, love." Her British accent soothed my nerves. "I didn't mean to startle you." She came to me and gave me a hug.

Her frailty in my arms surprised me. My breath caught in my throat, and I hugged her less tightly, afraid I'd hurt her. Martha is in her sixties, ten years older than me, though I've never known her to be fragile. Grief does terrible things to a body.

"I'm happy to see you," she said, stepping away from me.

"Me too. I'm so sorry for everything you're going through."

Martha headed toward the kitchen. The mess didn't shock her, so I presumed she'd already seen it.

The ballroom, kitchen, and living room—the social center— were open concept with a wide doorless threshold between the ballroom and the other two. I'd always been envious of Martha's home.

"I won't deny it," Martha said over her shoulder. "Having your entire world blown up is no barbecue. I know *you* know what I mean."

I *did* know. I leaned the broom against the round table and fell into step behind her.

As she left the ballroom, Martha said, "Hey, Jeeves. Turn on the kitchen light." She wasn't talking to me. She was talking to her smart home. After a momentary pause, the lights came on. "Have you coaxed the girls out yet, or are they still hiding?"

"I tried calling them, but I haven't seen them yet."

"It's been chaotic around here. It doesn't surprise me at all that they're hiding. The girls miss Harold. They were always more his babies than mine."

"I understand. I'll spend plenty of time with them while I'm here. Make sure they know they're loved. I imagine they're also freaked out by whatever made all this mess."

Martha halted, put her hands on her hips, and surveyed the kitchen and living room. "Yes. I'll have cleaners come in and take care of it."

"Don't do that, Martha. I'll clean it up. It'll give me something to do."

Martha stared at me. "Oh, heavens no, love."

"You know me. Cleaning is my preferred drug. And it'll be easier on Smaug and Faffy."

"You're a gentle soul, Kitty Kats. And a good friend. I'll make it up to you."

We shared tender smiles.

I asked, "What happened? Who did this?"

"It's a mystery. They found it like this, when they found... Harold." Martha hobbled to the kitchen island and rested against it. As if on cue, her cats appeared there, meowing in plaintive tones. "There's my girls." Martha slapped the island a couple times, and the cats leapt up. The ensuing love-fest was impressive.

Martha explained, "They're allowed on the island but not on the other countertops. They know. They'll behave."

I moved closer so I could join in with the petting. "Do you mind if I ask? How did Harold die?"

"Bad food."

"He had a heart attack? Diabetes?"

"No." She bent to touch her forehead to Smaug's back. The cat arched up against it. "I mean—literally—bad food. The police say it was botulism."

"Food poisoning? Oh dear! I'm so sorry! What did he eat?"

"Who knows? You know how Harold was. He'd put anything in his mouth."

"So...it wasn't murder? When you called me, you said..."

"I was a bit loony that day. The police believe it was an accident. Who am I to argue?" She sent her pale gaze around the room. "But look at this disaster. It's almost as if..." She trailed off.

"Someone was looking for something."

"If only I hadn't gone to visit my sister for a long weekend. I left Friday and got back Sunday evening. You can't imagine the scene I walked into, what with the police crawling all over the house and yard. The caretaker found him only hours before I returned. Good thing, that. I wouldn't want to be the one..."

I understood that. I'd been the one who found Bob. I wouldn't wish that on anyone.

"Had Harold been ill?"

"You saw the master bedroom already?"

I nodded.

Faffy, the plush Birman cat with cobalt-blue eyes and creamy fur, pushed her face under my hand, demanding more love. I obliged. She had always been my favorite because she purred the loudest. When she was happy, she let you know it. And when she wasn't—well—watch out!

"Harold fell on the terrace stairs and broke his hip. They gave him a new one. He was recuperating, and the doctors said he'd be fine as soon as it healed." Martha inched along the kitchen island, tidying as she went.

I was already having a hard time reconciling the state of the house with Harold's death being an accident.

"Could Harold have done this?" I gestured at the shambles.

"I doubt it. He couldn't stand for more than a few minutes. He still had a catheter. His caregiver came every day to check on him."

"Who's the caretaker?" My interest was piqued.

Martha rolled her eyes up, thinking. "Some young woman. She was kind and seemed honest." Martha raised her index finger. "I know what you're thinking, but I don't believe she's responsible."

"Who was it?"

"I don't remember her name. I only met her once. Harold hired her. I know she lives in Wyrdwood. I think she's a lar."

"A what?"

"You know. A lar. Descended from some household guardian lineage. Common as fleas in a doghouse."

"Oh." I studied her. "Martha? On the phone, you said Harold had been murdered."

"I was just upset and confused. I get that way...sometimes." She tapped her temple. "Early onset and all that. You know what I mean."

I knew, and it broke my heart that Martha was going through that. I had an aunt who had suffered from dimension. It was painful to watch, and I could only imagine how it must feel to be its victim.

She pushed off the island and turned toward the patio doors. "I need to get papers from Harold's office. Our executor is asking for them." She unlocked and tugged the sliding glass door open, using both hands and her full body-weight. "They tell me my husband loaned a man some money."

"Isn't Harold's office up here?" I pointed to the foyer.

"No. This way."

The terraced patio descended to the wide rocky beach, beyond which the lake sparkled in the afternoon sun. A forest of ancient pine and cedar trees wrapped the lake in giant green arms. The view always took my breath away.

Stone stairs connected each of the four levels. Martha hugged the metal railing as she descended them.

My Bob is standing by the grill, red-faced from the heat as he flips burgers and turns hot dogs. Our eyes meet, and he toasts me with his beer. I'm holding baby Diana in my arms, her body warm against my breasts. I am overcome with happiness and love. My husband. My daughter. Gratitude overwhelms me, and tears come to my eyes.

Martha's Harold says, "All right, lovebirds. Stop making bedroom eyes at each other and give me my hamburger!" We all laugh.

I followed Martha to the sliding glass door and, as I stepped out of the house, my toe caught on the sliding-door rail. I lurched forward. With the open staircase in front of me, I went off-balance. I took a clumsy step, then another, and somehow managed to catch myself. I avoided falling down the stairs and taking Martha with me. I clutched the railing and took a moment to reorient myself.

"Are you all right?" Martha looked back at me, concern on her face.

"Yes. Just cursed."

"You should do something about that." The come-back was a ghost of Martha's sense of humor. It was so spooky to hear that I didn't even laugh.

We continued our descent. The patio furniture was still covered, hibernating well into Spring. Martha's bulbs were just beginning to bloom—daffodils, crocuses, and tulips. The irises were stretching sleek shoots upward, preparing to bud in the coming weeks. I remembered the terrace as a party of color and laughter. Despite the flowers' efforts, without Bob and Harold, it felt cold and dead.

I said, "I don't remember a room back here."

"Harold had it built about five years ago or so. I wanted a guest room, and this was the solution. He moved his office down here."

The office occupied the space under the master bedroom. The upstairs balcony hung over it like the brim on a baseball cap.

Martha unlocked the door with a code. I accidentally saw her enter it and tried to forget it. How could I, though? It was 0407. The fourth of July.

Martha pulled open the door, reached to turn on the overhead light, and froze. She cursed under her breath.

I stopped on the threshold and echoed her curse.

The office was a stereotypical man-cave, seven feet from floor to ceiling. Its one window overlooked the lake but would never know direct sunshine. The intruder had ransacked the room to within an inch of its life. They had turned out drawers in every filing cabinet, and the floor was a sea of paper. The desk lamp lay on its side, and someone had forced open the locked desk drawer.

I could smell Harold's favorite cigars.

"Harold used to work in here?" In my head, I heard my daughter Diana preaching about wasted paper and evolving into the Digital Age. If she saw that office, she'd have blown a gasket.

"Every day," Martha said. "This was where he met with his crew."

"His crew?"

"Yeah, he was running some kind of contracting business on the side. Landscaping, he said."

"He was always busy, wasn't he?"

"He sure was. I'd have liked more vacations, but his work always got in the way."

Vacations with my Bob had ceased once Diana was grown, and I nodded with a large dose of sympathy.

Martha heaved a sigh and crossed to the desk. "How will I find those papers?"

I followed her. "Martha, you don't know who could've done this?"

"Not a clue." She shuffled through the papers on the desk. Her back hunched over, and her arms shook.

"Here, sit down." I moved the desk chair closer. She didn't object, and I guided her frail body onto the seat. "Can I get you a glass of water or anything?"

Martha had stopped blinking. "This is how our beautiful life ends," she said, her voice a hair above a whisper. "In chaos and destruction. I never knew the foundation was so rotten, the structure so fragile. I was blind. One second I was as happy as ever, and the next, I was destroyed. Everything I loved about my life. Gone. It was all an illusion."

I put my hand over hers. Her fingers were freezing cold. I thought I knew how she felt.

◆ ◆ ◆

CHAPTER 3

MUSE *smells his nemesis.*

Heavy is the tail that wears the crown. I am Muse. Being the king of cats in exile sucks. Sometimes, I wish I could be someone else, some other cat, like my courtier Greta—blissfully ignorant of the intricacies of the world. Her day revolves around food, naps, and tongue-baths. She has no idea what it's like to have a nemesis.

We all have to eat the kibble we're dealt, don't we?

I *am* what I am, and there's nothing I can do to change that. No more than my nemesis can change the fact that he's a pile of dog turds.

When I first captured his scent, it was like finding a single thistle in a field of spring flowers. It was a bad omen but not quite a warning. You can pee on the weed and hope it doesn't come back. But thistles spread underground, and before long, they overwhelm everything. They destroy all that is sweet and lovely about the world.

I had marked my territory too well, so it was inevitable that my nemesis would close in. He and I had danced that dance many times before. In the past, I'd always sent him running. This time, however, I wasn't so confident. I'd become a fat and lazy cat, sleeping on soft pillows and eating food that came from a can. I hunted occasionally, yes, and I usually caught my prey. But, eat it? Gross. Raw mouse doesn't compare to meat mousse served on a silver platter.

So, I usually just offer my kill as a gift to my minions. They never appreciate it. Whatever. It isn't about them. It's about *me*—my prowess. Bow to your better, humanoids.

Just joking. Sorta. It does thrill me to hear them gasp when they find my furry gifts. It's even more amusing when they step on them. And the prissy way they remove the corpses is absolutely adorable.

My Greta came to live with us and taught me a new way of living—the house-cat lifestyle. Greta's an excellent teacher. Leads by example. And I confess I grew to love her. She turned *my* days into ones of food, naps, and tongue-baths. It was luxurious, and I was loath to give it up.

I presumed Greta's people would want her back eventually, and so I plotted to hide her when the time came. If they couldn't find her, they couldn't take her.

◆ ◆ ◆

CHAPTER 4

DIANA *spies on miners.*

Eagle and I observed the miners from behind a basalt boulder. The cave we'd found had a high ceiling with a few prehistoric stalactites hanging from it. The icicle-like decorations made the place whimsical and thorny. The air was chilly enough that I could see my breath, and it smelled like a downpour after a dry spell—the heady aroma of wet rock.

In a narrow ravine below us, an underground river emerged from a hollow in the rock and flowed steadily through the chamber. It had eroded a winding path into the cavern floor. The water's surface shone black as obsidian, with golden highlights under the light from the miners' industrial lamps.

The miners were there, about half a football field away from us. Five of them. They had piled broken stalactites and stalagmites to divert a section of the river through their device. The machine vacuumed up river water and silt, filtered it, and spit the water out the other end. It made a horrendous noise that echoed in the cavern.

The miners regularly checked the filter, harvesting whatever they thought was valuable. Gold, undoubtedly.

"They're suction dredge mining," Eagle told me. "The water carries gold from inside the mountain, and they are collecting it."

"There's gold here?"

"Must be, or they wouldn't be here." Eagle pointed to a wooden shed the miners had built. In front of it, folding lawn chairs circled a metal fire pit. A pile of trash lay beside the shed. "This operation has been here for a long time." He took a few pictures with his digital camera.

"Are they breaking the law?"

"Not exactly. The state doesn't protect this river. Hell, these people have probably been doing this for years, maybe decades. No one knew they were down here until recently."

The machine turned off, and the place went silent. The stark difference was chilling.

"Whoa," I said.

Eagle put his index finger to his lips and whispered. "It echoes in here."

The miners left their positions and headed for the shed. They moved as if choreographed, or as if they'd done the same thing a thousand times. It was lunchtime. One lit a fire inside a metal ring, and they sat around it on the lawn chairs. Another handed out sandwiches, and another provided bottled beverages.

A female miner said, "...starving." Her voice carried to us, though it was distorted. She was bundled in a thick canvas coat, a wool hat, and padded work-pants, so I hadn't even realized she was a woman. Like the others, she wore thigh-high wading boots.

One of the men doubled over in a coughing fit.

"Dude...care of that," another miner said. He was tall, slim, and had the shadow of antlers hidden by magick.

I gasped, recognizing him.

Eagle put his hand over my mouth and glared at me. I pulled the hand away and glared back.

I knew Hunter Herne. We'd gone to high school together.

The Hernes all descended from the OG Herne the Hunter,

and they loved the chase. My mother had warned me about them when she'd discovered that I had a classmate from that family.

"Sometimes," Mom had said, "their prey is two-legged and pretty."

"I thought those were dogs." I chuckled, but Mom didn't get the joke.

"No, honey. The Hernes have stag antlers. That doesn't mean they have any connection to the animal itself. They see everything as a conquest, including beautiful young ladies like yourself."

"Oh, Mom!"

Of course, I hadn't listened to her, and when I was seventeen, I fell hard for a Herne. His name was Hunter Herne IV, named after his father, his grandfather, and his great-grandfather. The great-great-grandfather, named *Forest* Herne, thought he was being clever when he named his son Hunter. Families! Am I right?

It's accurate to say that Hunter Herne snagged me. Taking my virginity was a point on his rack, and I learned the hard way that people sometimes lie when they tell you they love you.

Hunter Herne the Fourth bragged about his conquest to the entire football team, who slapped him on the back and hooted his accomplishment. He was winning the race. I was collateral damage.

Manny Ortiz, one of my neighbors and my first crush, told me what Hunter had done. Manny was a cheerleader and had heard the locker-room crowing. Manny had taken it upon himself to inform me. He'd asked me how I could be so stupid. I wished I'd known the answer.

So, my first sexual experience—so monumental to me—was just another conquest to Hunter Herne. My rumor-mill celebrity lasted less than fifteen minutes because Hunter raced on, chasing other girls.

For the rest of the school year, I did my best to foil his hunt by warning his targets. Most of the time, I failed. My words fell on deaf ears. His prey knew how he was and didn't care. They all thought they were the one who would change him. Prince Herne told more girls he loved them than a princess kisses frogs.

As for me, I rejected all other advances until college. I told myself I was too mature for high school boys, but the truth was…I was scared. I couldn't go through that kind of shame again. Unbeknownst to me, my future husband would mastermind a Ponzi scheme and bring about my *greatest* humiliation. I was doomed. *He* was in prison.

"I need to get closer," Eagle whispered. "Stay here."

I followed him to another outcropping, mimicking his sneaky moves.

He hunkered down, and when I tucked in next to him, he gave me a side-eyed glare.

I made a gesture that said, *What?*

Closer like that, we could hear the miners better. I pulled out my phone to record them.

"Five hundred bucks, it cost me," one of them said.

"Ouch."

"Did they find the clog?"

"Yeah."

"Then I s'pose it was worth it. Don't imagine you liked having your shit bubbling up in your basement."

"It's highway robbery. It took two guys thirty minutes. That's two-hundred and fifty bucks each."

"Sucks."

"Next time, maybe you should do it yourself. See how that works out for you."

"Maybe I will."

"Look, it ain't that simple. It's expensive to run a business. Hell, even keeping this crappy equipment running costs money. If it weren't for the boss, we'd never be able to do it."

"Speaking of which, when's our take from that last haul coming?"

"Soon. Don't you worry. It's coming soon."

"How much you think we're gonna get? The river's been dry lately. I got bills, y'know?"

"Yeah. I got plumbers."

"Dude. We're gonna make enough to pay a hundred plumbers. It's just gonna take time."

"Speaking of which, back to work."

The afternoon dragged by. I fell asleep.

In the dream, I was a police detective. I'd just solved the crime no one else could, and my coworkers were applauding as I entered the station. My mom was there, and so was my dad. I could see my ex, Kyle, staring out from behind cell bars—like in an old Western.

I humbly waved them all off and went to see my boss, Chief Deputy Nick Harding.

I knocked, and he called for me to enter. He was leaning against his desk with a praising smile on his face. His office was freezing cold.

"Shut the door." I could see his breath.

"What's my next case, Boss?"

When I turned to close the door, I felt him step up behind me, right into my personal space. I could feel the heat wafting off his body in the chilly room.

"You deserve a reward, Detective Diana." His voice was low, right next to my ear. "Diana," he repeated.

"Diana?" Nick, my boss, shook me.

Then, it was Eagle who was shaking me. He was whispering, "Diana, wake up."

I sighed and opened my eyes. "What?"

"You were snoring," he whispered.

"Don't be ridiculous."

"The miners have finished for the day. They're packing up."

I'd fallen asleep against the basalt outcropping and was chilled to the bone. I wrapped my arms around myself and tucked my hands in my armpits.

"How long was I out?"

"Couple hours."

"What?" Because I had to whisper, I exaggerated my facial expression to express my surprise. "Did anything happen?"

"More of the same. Except one of them found something. They all cheered when he showed it to them."

That explained the applause in my dream.

"A gold nugget?"

Eagle grunted in the affirmative. He put a finger to his lips to shush me.

The miners pulled their vacuum out of the river and stowed their tools in the shed. Then, they gathered around a makeshift table to weigh their loot. An explosion of cheering and high-fiving echoed in the chamber.

The Herne wrapped their treasure up and stowed it in his backpack. Together, they trudged downstream, following the river bank until they were out of sight.

I gave Eagle a dry look. "There's another path out?"

"Of course."

"So I don't have to go back through that tunnel."

"Nah." Eagle gave me a crooked grin.

My mouth fell open and my nose wrinkled. "Why'd we come in that way?"

"To avoid the miners."

I tried hard to find something to be mad about, but was failing.

Eagle said then, "Was kinda fun, right?"

"Excuse me? There was nothing fun about it. I'm freezing, and I could eat a whole cow. Can we please get out of here?"

"Sure."

I stood up, stiff and sore from sitting so long on the cold rock. We scrambled down to the river and followed the miners, weaving our way out. I was relieved to see a sunshine-lit gap ahead, and I made a beeline for it.

The entire way, the memory of that dream plagued me.

Not a dog. Stop sniffing my rear-end.
— bumper sticker

◆

CHAPTER 5

KITTY *fumbles everything.*

Have I mentioned that I'm cursed? In a recent encounter with one of my son-in-law's Ponzi scheme victims, the man *cursed* me. I can't blame him. His poor mother had lost everything. What he didn't understand was that I was a victim, too. My husband had invested in Kyle's business.

I accompanied Martha to her car. She hadn't found the papers she needed, so to keep her from having a heart attack, I told her I'd keep an eye out for them. As I watched her get into the driver's seat, I boggled that the DMV even allowed her to drive. Her hands shook, and she employed choreography to get in. First, she clung to the frame and lowered herself backward into the seat, then she slowly—oh so slowly—placed first one foot then the other in under the steering wheel. Then, she had to find her keys.

I shut her door for her.

Martha turned the ignition and rolled down her window. "Give my love to Bob, won't you?"

My heart gave an achy thuh-dump-dump. Martha knew Bob was gone. She'd been at the funeral. I didn't know what to say, so I faked a smile.

Martha put the car in gear and started forward. She cranked the wheel in my direction. She didn't even notice I was in her path. Her wheel rolled toward my foot.

I stumbled back.

That morning's rain had made a muddy hazard of the driveway, and I slipped. As Martha drove off, I fell. Onto my back. In a puddle.

Martha didn't notice.

I rolled over and got to my feet. "I am *so* cursed." I stood there, dripping, and gazed up at the crystal blue sky. Another memory hit me square in the heart.

Bob comes out of the lake, dripping wet. He picks me up like I'm a child, holds me against his chest, then walks back into the water. My new sundress is soaked through, but I don't care. I cling to him and mock-scold him. I fall in love all over again.

I wasn't hurt, but I did have to maneuver my way inside, strip out of my muddy clothes by the front door, and walk through the house in my socks and underwear. I showered then put on clean clothes.

The guest bedroom was a mess. I shoved the mattress into place and put clean linens on the bed.

Martha's girls came into the guest bedroom to watch me. Smaug and Faffy sat on the bed together and bathed.

"Look at you, pretty babies. Thank you for keeping me company."

They glanced at me then went right back to bathing.

Once I was dressed again, I inserted the drawers in the bathroom cabinets and replaced their contents. I had no idea where Martha kept things, so I did the best I could.

"Someone," I told the kitties, "was searching for something. I bet they scared you, didn't they? Poor babies. You've had a rough week, huh? First your daddy dies, and then someone tears up your house. What do you suppose they wanted?"

By then, Smaug and Faffy had curled up in fur-puddles on the new bedding and were happily pretending to nap. Of their four eyes, only one cracked open at my question. I took that to mean they had no idea.

On my way to the kitchen for a cup of tea, I banged my shin on an overturned chair. That stung. It brought tears to my eyes. I hobbled around in a circle, cussing at my curse and walking off the pain. Eventually, it subsided.

The kitchen required even more tidying. Someone had dumped the food from the freezer into the sink. The searcher had left it there to melt. Nothing smelled bad—surprisingly—until I discovered an old canning jar of tomatoes. The lid bulged on it, and when I opened it to release the gases, it squirted tomato juice onto the counter. The funk of decay twisted my stomach.

The seal had been broken, and I wondered if that was the spoiled food that had poisoned Harold. I dug around for a freezer baggy, slid the jar into it, and put it in the freezer. I planned to hang onto it in case the sheriff's department wanted it.

Poor Harold.

I did a thorough sanitizing of the counters and sink. The last thing I wanted was for a curious cat to jump up on the counter and lick the botulism off their paws. Cats are as susceptible to food poisoning as humans are. If you come across a can of wet food with a broken seal, toss it out.

An hour passed by before I finally had my cup of tea in hand. I carried it to the sliding glass door, intent on relaxing on the terrace. Smaug appeared at my ankles and rubbed them. She wanted to go out too.

"No, honey," I told her. "There are predators who would love to sink their claws in a tasty morsel like you. Owls and eagles, cougars and trolls. Trust me, pea, you're safer inside. I'll be right back. I need a minute." I squeezed out, blocking her from bolting—and careful not to trip again.

The fresh air coming from the northwest was intoxicating. It was a mix of ocean, pine, cedar, and cut-grass. It dried my hair and pinked my cheeks. I welcomed the balmy coolness of it.

Martha and I are sitting together at an iron patio table, drinking tea. The deciduous trees are changing color, and there's a nip in the air.

Martha says, "Harold's going to leave me."

"No, Martha. Harold would never do that."

"I can't have children, Kitty." She bursts into tears. "I wouldn't blame him if he left me. It's easier for men. He can

still have a child with someone else."

"Harold loves you. I'm so sorry you can't have kids, but the only way Harold is leaving you is if you kick him out or if he dies."

Every corner of the Fishgiven home held memories for me. I inhaled and let it out slowly. My shoulders relaxed.

I'd been looking forward to staying at Martha's. I needed peace and quiet. The memories were a welcome part of that. It had been seven months, and I still hadn't completely processed Bob's death. I was glad to remember happier times. With my daughter living in my house with me, I could barely think, much less process. I was grateful for the chance to get away for a short while.

I love my daughter, but she never sits down—nor shuts up.

She had taken me on as her latest project. She told me at every opportunity how I could be more frugal, efficient, and careful. Our mother-daughter roles had gotten reversed, and I was beginning to understand why teenagers were so irritable.

The sun was setting in the west, casting a golden glow upon the lake. The view took my breath away. Birdsong and the buzz of hummingbird wings added music. I could have stayed there forever.

Then, the naked woman walked out of the lake.

◆ ◆ ◆

CHAPTER 6

MUSE *remembers his golden years.*

I curled up on an overstuffed armchair and contemplated my ghosts. As a scholar in my kingdom once said, "The past haunts you, the present tortures you, and the future menaces you." The scholar was a pessimist, but he wasn't wrong.

Once upon a time, I was the king of my kingdom. In my native language, the kingdom's name means, "The Place Where Whiskers Grow Long and Strong." For brevity, let's call it the Whiskers Kingdom.

I know I don't look it, but I'm beyond old. We don't need to get into exact numbers, but I remember when they transported Wyrdr Towne from what was the Kingdom of Scotland to Oregon. Is truth. It happened after my enemies dethroned me and banished me from our realm. I'd taken shelter in Wyrdr, so when they uprooted the entire town—cobblestones and all—and transported it using magick, in one piece, to the new world, they brought me along for the ride. Lucky them.

I'll never forget that day. I had no warning. I was dethroned and depressed. I had to sleep in filth and scrounge for food. I couldn't communicate with anyone. Not Normal cats. Not kith. It was a treacherous and lonely time. I was at my lowest point.

Then, one Spring day in the eleventh century, the ancient Fates wrapped an area six-kilometers-square, separated it from northern Great Britain, and *pop!* set it down on the coast of Oregon. Ta-dah!

To say that Wyrdwood "didn't fit in" is an understatement. Back then, Oregon was wild. The natives were unlike any people we'd ever encountered. Not all our interactions with them were peaceful. They called us many unflattering names because they feared us. We had arrived in one coup—one minute not there, next minute there, a wart on the beautiful cheek of Oregon.

Unbeknownst to history books, we were the first wave of Europeans to invade their territory. The difference between us and the later waves was that we had no interest in ousting them. Nor did we bring disease with us.

All we wanted was to hunker down in a corner of their world and hide. You might say we were refugees. Just like every European who arrived after us.

Over time, we established an uneasy peace with the natives. Wyrdwood settled in, eroded, and become as natural a part of the surrounding hills, mountains, and seashore as any native village might be. We began to trade with the locals, interbreed, and commingle our society with theirs.

We learned that there were kith among them as well, nature-spirit lineages that were as powerful as our own. In some cases more so, because the natives tended to believe in magick.

I acclimated to the new location, figured out which predators to avoid, and learned to understand the native language—although I couldn't speak it. I regained a portion of my dignity. In the new world, people smelled more like people and less like flowers. Flowers smelled more like flowers and less like chemistry. And food tasted like whatever you'd just killed.

It took the Europeans another five hundred years before they found us again.

It took Old Tom even longer.

Old Tom—my best courtier, my most trusted advisor, and my BFF—is a sophisticated short-hair with seal-point coloring. He's almost as handsome as I, or was, in his day. Much older than I, he had guided me through many rough situations while I was on the throne.

He doesn't live in Reality, but we get together on occasion to bask in moonlight together.

I'd been thinking about him since the fire at my previous residence. It occurred to me that he couldn't find me.

I was halfway through that thought when I fell asleep. Old Tom would have understood.

❖ ❖ ❖

CHAPTER 7

DIANA *finds a better exit.*

I'd have seen it coming if I hadn't been so obsessed with the weird dream I'd had. A part of me was mad that Eagle had woken me before I could get my reward. Another part was glad, because Nick was my boss, and I had no business having a kissy dream about him. Of course, the reward could have been chocolate. Or a raise? Maybe it was Eagle's sexy whisper in my ear that had turned the dream steamy. Either way, I concluded, I didn't need any complications. None.

Before I reached the cave exit, something lunged out of the shadows at me with a terrifying scream.

I automatically cringed and covered my face.

Eagle automatically punched the screamer. In the face.

My attacker went down and stayed down. It was a miner. If the urine stain on the rock wall was any indication, he'd lagged behind to attend to personal business in a rocky alcove.

"So, that happened." I stood up with effort, my muscles tense.

Eagle took hold of me and started moving me toward the opening. "C'mon. We need to get out of here."

"Wait!" I resisted. "Is he dead?"

"If I'd wanted him dead, he'd be dead."

I gave Eagle a wry look and said, "Oog."

The man was breathing, unconscious, with an angry blush on his jaw where Eagle had clocked him. Though he wasn't big, he had a sinewy build with limbs that were too long—gawky—as if he hadn't grown all the way into them.

"We can't leave him here." I knelt beside him. "What if he gets hypothermia? It'd be our fault."

Eagle rolled his eyes. "He's been wading in ice-cold river water all day."

"That's what I'm saying!"

Though he hesitated, Eagle came over and picked the guy up, tossing him over his shoulder in a firefighter's carry. "Keep an eye on him. If he starts waking up, warn me."

"Sure." I followed them up the steep incline. By the time we got to the top, I was out of breath. "Dang," I huffed. "I'm...out...of...shape. Huh."

"Not for long. Not if you stick with me." Eagle set the unconscious miner down on the path. "Time to go."

A voice shouted, "Darrel!" Nearby.

Eagle and I turned to see a man coming up the path. I guessed that the not-yet-dead man lying at my feet was Darrel. Quick-draw Eagle grabbed me by the wrist and launched himself (and me) in the opposite direction. In the split second before my feet left the ground, however, my eyes locked with those of the approaching miner.

It was their leader. My first love. Hunter Herne. His eyes had a golden gleam. Though he had shed his horns, the residual magick of his stag antlers was visible. He was magnificent—and terrifying.

Black, white, yellow, and brown are the mundane colors of race, the colors of Normal human races—variations in shade with pink mixed in. That is what Normals see. The multiverse is much more diverse, however. Races come in every color of the rainbow. Green. Blue. Purple. Red. Even orange. The Herne had olive skin—as did all his kin. They were forest beings. Fierce. Vengeful. Demanding. The descendents of Herne—and I'm generalizing here—do not appreciate others invading their territory.

"Hi," I said to him, even as Eagle was pulling me away.

The Herne pointed at me. Well, he pointed a gun at me.

Eagle jerked me, and I had no choice but to run to keep up.

A loud bang echoed off the rock, and a tree trunk near me spewed bark in my face.

We ran and ran, through the trees, down the ridge, across a stream, and along a deer path. We didn't stop until we'd reached Eagle's car.

As if he were afraid I'd fall over if he let go, Eagle took me to the passenger side and stuffed me into my seat. He slammed the door, and the only sounds I heard were the wheeze of my breath and the thunder of my heart.

Eagle had the car started before he'd even shut his door, and then we were backing out of the parking spot. He hit the accelerator, and the car spewed gravel.

I saw Hunter Herne standing at the treeline, his expression hard as stone.

Uh oh. We were in trouble.

◆ ◆ ◆

CHAPTER 8

MUSE *stares down his nemesis.*

Unaware that I was being watched, I claimed the window seat to bask in a ray of sunshine. I stretched and preened, the sun warming my fur. It felt so right.

Until it felt wrong. My hackles twitched, sensing the problem before any other part of me.

Scratch. That was his name, and there he was, sitting on the lawn outside, staring a challenge at me.

I first met Scratch when I was kittenish, a prince in need of a kingdom. My father wore the crown. Even then, Scratch and I had conflicted like tongue nubs stuck in long fur. We were natural competitors, both of us, and he never understood why I always bested him. I tried to tell him it wasn't his fault. Nor was it mine. I was genetically superior. That only made him angrier, for some reason.

By the time we'd buried my father and I'd ascended to the throne, Scratch had become my nemesis. He undermined my popularity, my authority, and my peace of mind. I had to have him thrown in prison, and well, that gave him a grudge he never got over. He worked from his cell, through his shady network, to destroy me. His plot was a success. My enemies framed me for a series of murders that I didn't commit, and the royal council members voted to oust me from the Whiskers realm. My scrawny cousin became the faux king.

In the end, Scratch had won. I had no choice but to slink away to Wyrdwood and go with them to the Oregon Territory. I had thought I'd never see Scratch again. Centuries had passed since my exile, and in all that time, I seen neither hide nor hair of him. And then there he was. On my lawn.

My back-fur bristled. So many times, I had fantasized about getting revenge on him. I, however, could not return to the Whiskers realm so long as the ban was in effect. Therefore, he'd been out of reach. He had done me a favor by coming to Reality where I could finally deliver his demise.

Scratch sat as still as a statue, except for the tip of his tail, which twitched back and forth, taunting me. Dust and mud obscured his gray tabby markings. One of his ears had the cauliflower folds of a bad ear-mite infection, and the other had a missing piece where I'd bitten him years earlier. He sneered at me, lifting one side of his upper lip.

Slowly, I turned, and step by step, inch by inch, I walked toward him... And thud! I ran into the window glass.

My nemesis flopped onto his back and rolled this way and that. Laughing at me.

Rage swelled up inside me. How dare he!

I sat and gave him an unblinking stare, imagining my claws slicing open that exposed belly.

Sorry. Too dark? Well, that's how I roll.

As fate would have it, an automobile pulled up at the curb. Diana got out. The demi-mistress was home.

I ran to the door.

The moment she opened it, I streaked out. Safety be damned! My pride was at stake. I was not going to let a trash-eater like Scratch laugh at me.

◆ ◆ ◆

> **The rose is fairest when 't is budding new,**
> **And hope is brightest when it dawns from fears;**
> **The rose is sweetest washed with morning dew**
> **And love is loveliest when embalmed in tears.**
> — Sir Walter Scott, "Lady of the Lake"

◆

CHAPTER 9

KITTY *meets a Lady of the Lake.*

I didn't mean to stare, but I was so confused. The woman who emerged from the lake was stark naked. Please understand. I'm no prude. In my day, I did my fair share of skinny-dipping. It wasn't her lack of clothing that troubled me. It was the fact that the water was still freezing cold. It was also the fact that she hadn't swum across the surface. She'd risen to the top from the depths.

I'd heard rumors all my life of the Ladies of the Lake, but never had I seen one. They were famous for being isolationists and interacted with the surface world only on rare occasions. They were all women—or so I'd been told. Speculation suggested they lived in the basalt caves that riddled the area. People claimed to have glimpsed the tops of great towers in the lake, glinting with golden trim. Still others surmised there was a portal to another realm under the water, an unimaginable realm where the Ladies made their home.

The Ladies of the Lake held dominion over the lake, though they didn't bother anyone who didn't dive too deep. The Wyrdwood Parks Committee had posted signs around the shoreline to warn off Normals and visitors:

DANGER.
Boat and swim only in clearly marked areas.
$5000 fine if caught in restricted waters.

It was for their own safety. Anyone who invaded the Ladies'

underwater territory ended up floating face-down.

The woman in front of me had beet-colored hair that must have been a glorious red when dry. It hung long and straight, curling only at the very ends. She wasn't much younger than me, though in Wyrdwood, a person could be a hundred and look fifty. Her body was natural and strong, with heavy motherly breasts, a poochy belly, and full hips. She was earthy and beautiful.

I expected her to walk along the beach, away from me, but she came toward me. When she got to the bottom floor of the terraced patio, she stopped. "I must speak with Harold."

I cleared my throat. "I'm sorry, but Harold—"

"I must speak with Harold."

"Harold isn't here. He passed away."

The woman's face fell, and her eyes dropped to the stairs. She breathed out and forgot to inhale again.

"I'm Kitty. What's your name?"

"Rhiannon," she said, without looking at me. I barely heard her.

"I can tell Martha you—"

"I'm Harold's wife."

I froze in a state of shock, unsure that I'd heard her correctly. Or maybe she didn't understand what that word meant. "His wife?"

The Lady of the Lake turned and walked back to the water's edge.

I rushed after her, one hand on the railing the whole time. Dang curse! I made it without face-planting, but Rhiannon was already entering the water.

"Rhiannon! Wait!"

She didn't wait. She just kept going until her hair spread like algae on the surface of the water. Then it too went under, and she was gone.

Harold had another wife? *What?*

I made myself a second cup of tea to help me relax. It wasn't helping, so I called Diana.

"Hey, Mom. What's up?"

"Hi, honey. You busy?"

"Always, but that never seems to stop you. Are you okay?"

"Always. But..."

"Mom. What's going on?"

"Honey, I found another mystery."

In the background, that yappy dog of Diana's was doing what it does best: yap. It had to do the only *other* thing it was good at: poop.

"Hold on, Mimi," Diana said. "We can go out in a minute."

"Do not," I warned, "let her poop in the foyer."

"Mom, she hasn't done that in days. I'm keeping an eye on her, and she's learning. What's the mystery?"

I took my tea and the phone into the living room. "I'm cursed."

"That's no mystery. We're all aware of that."

"I'm serious, Di! That man, the one I told you about, put a curse on me."

"You mean Mr. Bowtie? I already apologized about that. He shouldn't be threatening *you*. It was *my* husband who stole his family's money."

"You weren't home, so he cursed me instead."

Diana sighed. "Okay, I'll bite. What makes you think you're cursed?"

"I almost died three times today."

"Don't be so dramatic."

"It's true. I almost fell down some stairs and almost got run over by a car. I fell in a mud puddle and might've drowned in it."

Diana asked wryly, "Do I need to worry about you?"

"Aaaand, you will not believe what just happened to me. I'm out here at Martha and Harold's place..." I paused to take a breath, and my daughter interjected, "I know where you are, Mom."

I continued, "I was standing on the top terrace. You remember Martha's terrace, right? In the back?"

"I remember."

"Well, I was just standing there, admiring the view, and this woman walks out of the water." I gave my words a dramatic cadence. "Newwwwwd as the day she was born."

"You're kidding?"

"No! It was a Lady of the Lake, Di. I swear it was."

"You sure it wasn't a lost tourist?"

"I'm sure. She was in her fifties, at least. Mature. But beautiful. Confident. She knew exactly where she was going."

"Okay."

"Anyway, she comes up to the house and asks for Harold. I told her he'd died. She was crestfallen."

"Crestfallen? Mom, who says that?"

"It means 'very disappointed.'"

"I know what it means."

"Sure. But get this part. She told me she was his wife."

"His life? What does that mean?"

"Not his Life. His Wife. Wife. As in, until death do us part."

"That's ridiculous, Mom. Was the woman delusional?"

"I don't think so, honey. She believed it. Maybe she meant 'ex-wife?' You can never tell with some kin. They have their own language sometimes."

I set my tea mug on the cluttered coffee table, then, one-handed, picked up a couch cushion and returned it to the sofa. "She didn't know Harold was dead." I sat down.

"Holy cow. I mean...it's Uncle Harold. I can't even imagine him with anyone but Aunt Martha. Didn't he meet Aunt Martha when they were kids?"

"Yes."

"There has to be some mistake. If this woman is a Lady of the Lake—"

"She is."

"Okay. The word 'wife' must mean something different in her culture."

"Maybe. Should I tell Martha?"

Once again, Diana gave me only silence.

I put my palm on my forehead. "I shouldn't. The last thing Martha needs is more chaos. I'll wait until she gets back from England. Then I'll mention it."

Diana suggested, "She might already know."

"Yeah, could be. But if she doesn't…"

"You're right. Better to let it slide for now. C'mere, Mimi."

Through the phone, I heard the familiar jingle of Mini-Mimi's leash. Despite her small stature, the Yorkshire Terrier could run faster than a cat with its tail on fire. Thus, the leash.

I said, "By the way, the police determined that Harold died of food poisoning."

"Really? That's awful."

"It is. I found a jar of tomatoes that turned. It might be what he ate. Do you think the police would be interested? I put it in a baggy and stuck it in the freezer for them."

"I don't know. Call and ask them."

"Who should I call?"

"Call the station and ask to speak to the deputy in charge of the Fishgiven case. They'll direct you."

"Can't you just ask for me?"

"Mom…" Diana sighed. "Okay, I'll ask around, see what I can find out."

"Thanks, honey." I had run out of things to talk about, so I brought it full circle. "What should I do about this curse?"

"Maybe go see a curse doctor?"

"There's no such thing."

"Well, why are you asking me? I have no idea."

"Did I mention I had another burst of magick today?" I paused then added, "Or, it might have been a hot flash."

"You don't do magick."

"I did do magick. During the fire, remember? I shrank my butt to get out the window." My very first use of magick had been a tiny fart of a spell. Unexpected. Yet, it had saved my life. Of course, because I am me, it had to involve shrinking my bottom.

Ever since I survived the fire, I'd been on high alert for something magickal to happen again. I couldn't wait to grow into a powerful dakini—my ancestral lineage. It happened to the women in my family, in our crone years—assuming we lived long enough. In the meantime, I was cursed.

"Mom, you're dragging this conversation out." Diana opened the front door. "I have to walk..." She dropped the sentence. After a moment, she cried, "Oh my god! Mom! Your cat's hurt!"

"What do you mean 'hurt?' Which cat?"

"Muse. He's bleeding. I think something bit him. He's breathing, but it looks bad. He's just lying there."

"Get him to the vet, honey. Use one of the empty cardboard boxes in the dining room. Call an e-taxi."

"I'll call you back, Mom."

And she hung up.

◆ ◆ ◆

CHAPTER 10

MUSE *goes to the vet.*

The veterinarian wanted to kill me, and the feeling was mutual. Yet, somehow, I'd ended up there. I remember bits and pieces. The smell of blood. The pain in my side. The vile taste of Scratch in my mouth.

My ears were still ringing with catfight opera.

I thought, "Just let me die..." and I tried to force out my last breath. Leaving this life in battle was honorable. And Scratch had gone limping into a ditch, so I claimed victory. Despite my wounds, my body kept inhaling again and again. Yeah, one of the drawbacks of being immortal.

I woke up in a throne, the quintessential royal bed—a cardboard box—with dry mouth and Diana's face looming over me. She said, "You're okay, buddy. I've got you." For a moment, I feared I'd croaked and gone to Cat Heaven. Then, Mini-Mimi barked.

The next few hours passed in a blur. I was jiggled and poked, drugged and puppeted. Fortunately, I was drugged, so I didn't know the true breadth of my humiliation.

By the time I woke up, it was the middle of the night. I was in a cage with a bowl of cheap kibble and a tiny litter box filled with shredded newspaper. There's nothing so nasty as wet paper under you while you're doing your business. It splashes, and it sticks to your toes.

They'd shackled me with a giant slave collar around my neck. I couldn't lick my...well, anything.

At least the water was cool and fresh. I drank my fill.

Strange music surrounded me. Growls, grunts, snores, and snuffles punctuated by clangs of metal. Something lapped water. A mystery creature scratched in a litter box. A tap-tap-tap-tap kept up a steady rhythm.

And the smells! Horrific waves of desperation, sweat, blood, and tears covered by the overwhelming stank of cleaning supplies. Chemistry. It offended my senses, and I was forced to breathe it. With the collar, I couldn't even cover my nose. I panted, inhaling as shallowly as possible without passing out.

I missed Kitty—her hands, to be specific. And her warm belly. Was she ever coming to get me? Did she even know I was there? I feared that cage would be my world evermore. I spiraled into dark thoughts. No Kitty. No Diana. No Greta. Oh, woe! No Greta!

No Mimi. There's a silver lining to every cloud.

Sleep eluded me. All I had to pass the time was the waiting, the hoping, and the thinking.

Why had I gone after Scratch? Why? He'd been on the verge of dealing my death blow when a broom hit him in the head. Someone had heard our caterwauling and come to fight at my side. Scratch wimped out. Shocker.

I was still high on adrenaline, so I ran off as well. Toward home. I made it as far as the porch before my strength left me. Diana found me there. I should be grateful that she—being a dog-lover—didn't just kick me into the bushes.

◆ ◆ ◆

CHAPTER 11

DIANA *returns home alone.*

Muse had a hissy-fit when I left him at the vet. Such a drama queen! If nothing else, his voice was healthy.

They were keeping him overnight to give him a chance to begin healing while under observation.

I called Mom from the e-taxi.

"Hey, Mom."

"Honey! Is Muse okay?"

"He will be. The dumbass got into a fight with a dog, or another cat, or maybe a gnome? I don't know, but it scratched him up pretty badly. The vet gave him a few stitches and antibiotics. They're keeping him overnight. If the volume of his complaining when I left is any indication, he'll be fine."

"Oh, poor baby. Should I come home?"

"No. I've got it. Besides, he's stuck at the vet until tomorrow. They'll call me when he's ready to leave. I'll go pick him up."

"Thank you, honey. I'll pay you back for the taxi rides. Poor kitten. I bet he's frightened to death."

"He'll be okay."

"Di, I'm glad you called."

I checked my mirror to change lanes, and Mom continued, "Something's not right here at Harold and Martha's. There's mischief afoot."

"What does that mean? Are you manifesting trouble where there is none?"

"No. You haven't seen this house, Di. Someone tore it apart searching for something."

I sighed. Before she could steer the conversation back to Harold's death, I signed off. "Gotta go, Mom. I'm almost home. I'll call you tomorrow when I go get Muse."

"All right, honey. I love you."

"Love you too, Mom."

As the e-taxi turned onto our block, my blood ran cold. An old red pickup sat in front of the neighbor's house. That wasn't a problem, but as I drove past it, I glanced over and saw one of the miners in the driver's seat—Hunter Herne.

Our eyes met as we rolled by. A slow smile spread onto his face, and he gave me a threateningly cordial nod.

I debated whether I should tell the driver to keep going or not, but Herne already knew where I lived. With one eye on him, I shot out of the car as soon as it stopped and ran to the front door.

Of course, I fumbled with my keys.

Herne didn't leave his truck. Just sat there, smiling at me.

I conquered the door and entered the foyer. My foot slipped on the tile floor, in something slick. I caught myself before falling. Thank goodness. But, when I checked, I discovered I'd stepped in dog poo and a puddle of piddle.

And there was Mimi, running back and forth, dragging her leash—which I'd left on her in my rush to save Muse. Through the mess. Back and forth. Smearing it like a Pollock painting. I'm not sure which was more horrifying, finding the miner outside my home or Mimi's artwork.

◆ ◆ ◆

CHAPTER 12

KITTY *fails to sleep.*

had to straighten the guest room before I could sleep there. I glared at the scattered clothes. Last thing I wanted was to get up to pee and trip on one of Martha's voluminous bras. I was so tired I didn't even bother making the closet neat. I rehung the shirts, skirts, and dresses already on hangers and stuffed the rest into a corner in a heap. I planned to deal with it the next morning.

Martha had moved into the guest bedroom when Harold broke his hip. It had its own full bathroom and decor in pretty shades of blue.

Harold and Martha were wealthy compared to me and Bob—compared to most people in Wyrdwood. Harold had always been lucky in business. He had an entrepreneurial spirit. He'd quit his last job while still a teenager. His boss had been an ogre who treated him like an afterthought. He swore then that he'd never work for anyone else. "Never again."

Despite this, neither he nor Martha had been showy about their wealth. They'd spent it on comfort, not luxury.

I found Martha's jewelry box tossed into a corner. It was full of beautiful, yet simple, pieces. Quality necklaces, rings, and bangles—all gold. The thief had rejected them.

I took a shower, put on my pajamas, and wrapped my hair in a towel. Martha's bed was a queen with plenty of room for me and the kitties. They scooted aside when I got in, letting me settle before approaching to say goodnight.

"Aw, you kittens are so sweet." I petted them.

Their kindness touched me, and a wave of grief swelled within me. Most days, I was better at keeping the tears at bay, especially in front of Diana. But the kindness of others always tore a hole in my walls. It started with a few tears swelling in my eyes. My heart ached. I had so many memories of Bob in the Fishgiven house. Laughing. Drinking. Watching the sunset from the balcony with his arm around my waist. I'd give anything to feel that again, to lean against his warm body, and smell his Old Spice.

"Oh, kitties," I whispered. "I miss him. And I'm scared." The tears came quicker. "It just hurts. It hurts so much."

I gave in to my sorrow, swam in happy memories, and petted the kitties' heads.

Until I fell asleep.

Something woke me in the night. I had one kitty between my knees and one draped over my hip. I lay there in a fog for a moment and then drifted back to sleep. I had just fallen into blackness when a noise roused me again. I'd heard something real. Both kitties were still on the bed, but they'd raised their heads and were watching the door.

My scalp crawled.

I started pulling back the covers, creeping, trying to be as silent as I could. Smaug and Faffy jumped to the floor. I slid out of bed.

The room had a chill, and the clock on the bedside table said it was 3:33 A.M. The witching hour. It was uncanny how often I woke up at that time.

I was listening with intent and heard a clunk from somewhere in the house.

Was it the thief?

Had Martha come back to search for the paperwork?

Maybe Harold's ghost?

To my dismay, the first one made the most sense to me. I decided to err on the side of caution. I tiptoed toward the bedroom door and started to close it. Before I could shut it, however, both kitties zoomed out into the ballroom.

I stood there, staring into the darkness after them. I wanted to lock the door between whoever was in the house and the three of us. Without the girls, I couldn't do that.

After a moment's debate, during which more rattling and

shuffling came from Harold's bedroom, I made a decision. I retrieved my phone from the bedside table and dialed 9-1-1. With the phone to my ear, I picked up one of Martha's hard-heeled dress shoes and held it by the toe, ready to hammer, if need be.

"Wyrdwood 9-1-1. Is this an emergency?"

I whispered, "Yes. Intruder in the house." I tried to say as much as possible in as few words as possible.

"All right, ma'am. What's your address?"

I gave it to her, and she read it back to me.

"Is this Martha Fishgiven?"

"No. Catsitter."

"All right. What's your name, ma'am?"

"Kitty Kats."

"Kitty Kats?"

"Yes."

"Ma'am, it's illegal to prank 9-1-1."

"Not a prank. Real name. Please. Send the sheriff."

The woman on the other end sniffed. "A deputy is on the way. Are you in the house?"

"Yes."

"Where, exactly?"

"Bedroom, southeast corner."

"Okay. Is the front door open?"

"No. It's locked. Alarmed."

Smaug wandered back into the bedroom, but Faffy was nowhere in sight. So, it wasn't Martha. If it had been, both cats would've been swirling around their mom's ankles.

The realization made my breath hitch.

The intruder had been silent for a time. All I could hear was my blood rushing through my veins.

"I can try to go to the door?"

"Stay where you are, ma'am. The deputies can get in."

I knew what that meant. They'd break down the door. I cringed at the idea.

Another shuffle from Harold's bedroom inspired me to lean out and peer in that direction. The moon was a waxing crescent, so there wasn't much light coming in from outside. A night-light in a wall socket provided some illumination, but it didn't reach into the bedroom.

The crunch of gravel outside announced the sheriff's vehicle. I wasn't the only one who heard it.

Someone streaked out of the bedroom and passed through the night-light's glow. His silhouette burned into my brain. He was tall and slender, and his hair had two cowlicks as if he had devil horns. He loped to the sliding glass doors in the kitchen, slipped outside, and ran down the stairs.

I bolted for the front door, turned off the alarm, unlocked it, and opened it just as the first deputy stepped onto the porch. We stared at each other, both startled.

I pointed. "He ran out the back!"

◆ ◆ ◆

CHAPTER 13

MUSE *flees Purgatory.*

A bided my time, trapped in Purgatory, purring away the pain. I must have fallen asleep because I awoke when a worker arrived and made a clatter. The sun was rising. The dawning light casting warmth against the enormous windows.

There, on the opposite side of the street, insolent cur that he is, sat Scratch. He didn't look any better than I felt. He stayed there for a while, menacing me, but he broke eye-contact first and limped away.

I was miserable. Not only was I caged with a giant cone collar, but my belly was freezing—as if I were bare-skinned there. Later, I would learn that was true. The vet had shaved around my wound. My fur, oh, my fur! No wonder I felt so weak. I was Samson, betrayed by Dr. Delilah. I doubted it would ever grow back, and I wailed my shame and sadness.

They tried to soothe me, but I howled in indignation. How dare they? Expose my tummy and sap my strength.

My cries wormed into their brains and undermined their peace. When they realized there was nothing to be done to shut me up, they called Diana. Before long, she walked in to save me.

I'd never seen such a beautiful rescuer. The moment she picked me up out of the cage, I fell madly, deeply in love with her and showed it. My purrbox kicked into high gear, and I clung to her as if my life depended on it.

She cuddled me while we both calmed down. Oh, Diana. My sweet. You are my hero!

Later, I'd realize it was a drug-addled overreaction, but in that moment, I was overcome with love.

I rode in a royal carriage, carried by Diana. The vet and his people smiled at me, waved, and coo-coo'd, but I ignored them. They did not deserve my love.

When we arrived at the house, it occurred to me that Greta would see me in my weakened condition. Fear rose into my gullet. A king must never show weakness.

Diana took me inside and set my royal carriage on the couch. She opened the door and tried to get me out. I did not want to go. I backed away and hissed at her.

"Oh, for heaven's sake," she said. "Fine. At your leisure, goofball. I'll get food and water ready for you."

I sat there. For an interminable amount of time. It must have been minutes! At long last, a whiskered face appeared in the doorway of my carriage. A beloved face. My Greta. She sniffed, taking in the aroma of me and the vet. I realized I had not bathed since before my battle.

Her soft mew coaxed me from my shelter. I couldn't look her in the eyes for fear of what I'd see there. I was a king! And I'd hit bottom. I was filthy and powerless to do anything about it because of that horrid collar.

Once I was out of the carriage, I sat on the couch cushion, taking my punishment with humility and my one remaining scrap of dignity. Any minute, Greta would hiss and run from me. I sensed her snoofing about, scenting me.

Then she licked me. My heart gave a big swollen thump, and a tear welled in my eye.

"Mom," said Diana in the kitchen. "I've got Muse. He's home. The vet said he'll be fine. We have to keep watch over him though. So he doesn't open his stitches."

I half-listened, soothed to semi-consciousness by Greta's ministrations. Bless her sweet face.

"An intruder? When? Jeez, Mom. Are you okay?"

She opened the refrigerator door. "No, you're not cursed. Stop saying that, or it'll become a self-fulfilling prophecy. You did the right thing. Do you know what they wanted?"

Halfway through Kitty's sentence, Diana put the phone on speaker. Kitty said, "...didn't take anything. I don't think they knew I was there."

"Well, I'm glad you're okay. I have a solution. It's Saturday. My boss called me into work, but why don't I come out there when I get off. I can bring the animals. I wouldn't mind a change of scenery."

Kitty said, "Hm. I *could* use your help cleaning this place up. It's topsy-turvy."

"Sure. I'll help. I owe it to Uncle Harold and Aunt Martha. Besides, I wouldn't mind a chance to meet a Lady of the Lake."

That caught my attention! The Ladies of the Lake were one of many reasons cats don't like water. Back in the old days—prehistoric times—cats loved water and the fish that swam in it. Then, we met the Ladies of the Lake. They didn't appreciate us eating their shimmery friends. So, they started killing us. Many a feline nursing rhyme warns kittens of the dangers of water. "That is not your kingdom," the mamas sing. "That is your death." Our fear has merged with our instincts, and most cats will do anything to escape water, even the shallowest puddle. Wet paws equal danger.

The Ladies of the Lake have always lived in the depths of fresh-water lakes.

Their relatives appear all over the world in all kinds of water. Some are more dangerous than others. I've heard them called Aloges, Loreley, Naiades, Grindylows, Leannan Sidhe,

Rusalka, Jengu, Mami Watas, Melusine, Sayonas, Shellycoats, Nokken, Kappa, Lloradas, and Water Sprites, among many other names. Some live in fresh water, some in salt water, some in swamps and brackish water, and some on land near water. Each is a branch of kin who descend from the goddess Tethys. The family tree's branches are each unique yet similar, as relatives are. Many have been forgotten, gone into hiding, or died off. Historians in my kingdom believe that even the dragons of lakes and oceans descend from Tethys.

The Ladies of the Lake are one branch of this diverse kin. Matriarchal in nature, the Ladies of the Lake prefer isolation, away from the landlubber world, except when they want to breed.

To have a child, they take surface-dwellers as lovers. They may raise male offspring, but they do not keep them past a certain age. They send them onto land because they believe that men cannot thrive in the element of water the way women can.

My thoughts had grown rambling. Greta continued to shloop-shloop. My eyelids drooped. And at last, I drifted off into merciful sleep.

◆ ◆ ◆

CHAPTER 14

KITTY *goes boating.*

Buried up to my ankles in papers, I did my best to make sense of the mess in Harold's office. I'd decided to start there and search for the paperwork Martha needed. I texted Diana so she'd know where I was when she showed up.

The kitties and I had already had breakfast, and I'd made coffee. I took a mug downstairs with me.

Harold had worked at the WYRD-TV news station for most

of his life, as an audio technician. It meant he traveled quite a lot, following news stories. Sometimes he was the man holding the camera, sometimes he was the one in front of it. He'd loved the spotlight, but he didn't have the looks to become an anchor. He used to say that news correspondence was where the real magick happened.

As a result, he was gone for days or even weeks at a time, depending on where they were sending him. Martha hated being alone for so long, but she would never have stood in his way.

Old newspapers covered the floor, mixed in with the files tossed out of Harold's filing cabinet. Harold had read the Wyrdwood Gazette every morning, as if it were his church. It appeared that he'd hoarded issues for years. I piled them in the corner, though I didn't bother to sort them by date. Chances were they'd get thrown out anyway.

My favorite thing about the Wyrdwood Gazette is the magickal insert. It has always amazed me how Normals see an advertising insert, whereas people like me, with magickal blood, see the special edition news.

When I was younger, I was addicted to the *Ask Miss Goose* column. I spent far too many Sunday mornings trying to figure out who wrote the letters asking for advice. Although it was a huge scandal, the fact that someone revealed Miss Goose's true identity never bothered me. Knowing it was Emmelina Gosbinner didn't take the fun out of it for me. I wanted to discover who was getting a divorce, or who hated their job, or who was celebrating their first shapechange. Because of Emmelina Gosbinner, Miss Goose, I discovered the joy of mysteries and word puzzles. And I loved to guess who the anonymous questioner was. I was talented at it—or so I thought.

A glint of gold appeared as I moved the papers aside, and I found a framed picture of a much younger Harold. He was dressed in adventure clothing and stood inside a vast cavern. Even as a young man, he hadn't been handsome, but there was something about him that was intriguing. Harold could be stoic and serious to the point of being cold. He had his opinions, for sure, but could be a charmer when he wanted to be. When he was playing host, he could turn a simple gathering into the party of the year. Everyone loved getting invited to the Fishgivens' home. He was a born entertainer. Still, there was stone under the fancy facade.

I sat at Harold's desk. More papers covered it, strewn about as if someone had rummaged through them. I was gathering them up, creating a neat stack, when I found a crumpled piece of stationery. It was gray paper with flecks of dried seaweed stuck in it. It was pretty. I spread it upon the desktop, smoothing out the wrinkles.

It said, "Harold, husband. You have broken our covenant. Three times, you have not appeared. Although it breaks my heart, I have no choice but to release you from my protection. It is our way. Rest assured that I will tell our children your name. At the new moon, we will no longer be married. Thank you for your many years of dedication." And it was signed, "Rhiannon."

Someone had balled it up. Harold? I can't imagine he was pleased to read it.

The sound of a boat engine rattled the windows, and a pontoon fishing boat pulled up to the Fishgiven dock with Elias Kariuki at the wheel. His bald head had a golden shine to it, and he appeared to be fit and happy. Out of his fire chief uniform, it was easy to forget he held such a prestigious position. He resembled a regular old weirdo coming back from fishing. His Hawaiian shirt displayed multi-colored flowers on a neon green background, and his knee-length nylon shorts matched the green.

I dropped the note from Rhiannon into the box and headed out to greet Eli.

"Hey!" I called as I walked along the dock. "That shirt is so loud, it's going to scare all the fish away."

He laughed and disembarked with a line in hand. "In my experience, the fish think we're having a party. It puts them at ease."

"Oh, what a cruel deception."

A breeze had kicked up. Between it and the sunshine, the day had become the perfect flavor of balmy. The smell of the lake carried with it a millennium of history, life, and nature. Just like that, my mood rebounded.

Eli knelt to tie the line to the cleat. His legs were even more brown than usual and muscled. He kept in shape. He was the kind of "active" that I'd been when I was twenty years younger. Somehow, he'd managed to avoid the recliner.

I was relieved to hear him grunt as he stood. He dusted off his hands and came toward me. "It's gorgeous out today, Gorgeous. I thought maybe you'd like to go for a boat ride?" He wrapped me in a hug before I could protest then proceeded to lift me off my feet.

I squeaked. I allowed myself a moment of basking in the feel of his strong arms around me. Only a brief moment. Then, I signaled that I wanted to be released.

Putting me down, he said, "I've been out since dawn. I've got veggies, cheese, sliced ham, and sub rolls. Fresh lemonade. We could have lunch on the water. What do you say?"

I stuck my teeth together and inhaled through them. "I can't today, Eli."

"Why not?" he asked with a patient smile.

"The way my luck is going, I'd fall overboard and drown."

Eli laughed. "Lucky for you, I've got enough luck for both of us." He moved to the edge of the dock and held out his hand to invite me aboard. "C'mon. Just an hour. I'll drive fast. Blow off that dark cloud that keeps following you around."

I frowned at him. "I don't have a dark cloud."

Both his eyebrows rose, and his smile spread. "It'll do you good." He kept his hand extended.

I gazed out at the sparkling surface of the lake. The sun warmed the top of my head and my shoulders. I loved boats. Truth was, he'd had me at 'Just an hour.' I could do that, and well, I wanted to, darn it. So, I took his hand and let him guide me across the gap and onto the boat.

He released the lines then joined me. "You won't regret it." He pointed to a cabinet under one of the benches. "Sunglasses, sunscreen, a sweater, and a life vest. Take any you feel you need. I'll get us underway."

I took a life vest and put it on. It smelled like the lake.

Eli asked, "How's Mrs. Fishgiven doing?"

"Not so well. Harold's death hit her hard. She's not her old self."

"I'm sorry to hear that."

"How'd you know I was catsitting for her?"

Sly Eli gave me a waggle of his eyebrows. "I know people who know people." He crossed to the helm, turned the key, and pushed the ignition button. Eli's baby was a pontoon boat designed for fishing. It had white sides and floor, and navy cushions on the chairs and benches. At the stern, a railed platform had two rotating seats. The outboard motor lived under a cover, hidden from sight. It purred like a kitten.

"You ready?"

"Ready!" My own grin surprised me.

Eli guided the boat away from the dock.

We made one lap around the large lake in silence. With the wind in my hair and the sun on my face, I forgot to be sad. Other boats floated on or sped across the lake, and Eli navigated with a respectable expertise, keeping his attention on the water the whole time we were moving. He stopped the boat in a beautiful spot off the main thoroughfare and turned back to me.

When he saw me, a broad grin spread across his face. Oh, what I must have looked like with my hair messy and my cheeks rosy. His were also sun- and wind-kissed. He sat on the bench opposite me and bent forward, elbows on thighs.

"Any clouds left?" His eyes sparkled. "We could go around again, if you need it."

I laughed. "No clouds left. Thank you. Turns out I did need that."

"I thought as much." He bent and opened a shallow hatch in the floor. Inside was a folding table that he removed. "Hungry?" He unfolded the table's two legs and inserted them into slots in the deck. The table stretched between us.

I'd forgotten how easy it was to spend time with Eli. He didn't talk much, but he said plenty. I felt no pressure to be entertaining. I could tell he was just happy to be there with me.

We ate the sandwiches and drank the strawberry lemonade he'd brought. The boat rocked, and I relaxed more and more.

"Remember that summer I saved up and bought old Blue-beard's skiff?"

"I remember you painted the name 'Kitten' on it."

"We spent every day on the lake."

"I don't think I've ever been that tanned." I leaned over the side and peered into the water. "Whatever happened to it?"

Eli chuckled. "I still have it. In my boathouse. It's still sea-worthy, believe it or not. After all these years."

Something in the water caught my eye. The sun was delving ten or twenty feet down, illuminating what resembled a pointed spire. It gleamed in counterpoint to the water's surface shine, and it was too perfect to be natural.

"Eli?" I asked. "What is that?" I got up on the bench, on my knees.

Eli joined me and leaned over the railing. "Ahhhh," he said. "The lake levels are dropping. All I know is that we were never meant to see it."

A loud speed boat zoomed by, so I had to wait a beat to ask my next question.

"The Ladies of the Lake?" I leaned farther to try to make out what it was.

"I don't know."

"It's not a natural structure."

"No."

At that moment, a wave from the speed boat hit the pontoon and rocked it.

I felt my bottom rise higher than my head, and gravity took hold of me. Off-balance, I flew up and then down, into the water.

"Kitty!" Eli made a grab for me but missed, so there I was, dumped into Lake Talyllyn over a magickal citadel.

Panic zapped me, and I swam as fast as I could back to the surface. The boat was gone! Another wave of panic overtook me.

I bobbed on the surface, my life jacket keeping me afloat.

Eli shouted, "Kitty!" And I realized I was facing away from

the boat. Duh. Once I turned, I relaxed and headed for it. The water was still frothy with waves from the speedboat. I got water in my mouth, and it tasted bluegreen.

"C'mon, girl," Eli stood on the stern, crouching and holding a hand out to me. "Ladder's here."

The life jacket made it harder to swim, but it saved my life.

I thought, *I am so cursed,* and in my head, I heard a child's laugh.

Something cold wrapped around my ankle and dragged me under.

"Kitty!" Eli's voice sounded so far away, and the sunlight's sparkle was growing dimmer and greener. The temperature dropped with each foot I descended.

The surface sparkled above, the sunlight streaking through the water around the outline of the boat.

I bent double and tried to unlatch whatever had hold of me. Fingers. A hand. A bloom of long, swaying hair the color of the lake's darkest depths.

My lungs started to burn. Then, just as suddenly, the being let go. I hung there for a moment, disoriented and shocked. Right in front of me was the apex of the spire. I could have reached out and touched it, if I'd wanted.

Carved from basalt, the rock was riddled with tiny holes where bubbles had gotten trapped in the volcanic flow. Perfectly symmetrical, it had artful spiraling curls chiseled into it, decorative currents or waves. The size of the spire hinted at how deep the water was. Below me, visibility dropped to nothing just below my feet, and my gut clenched. My captor—my murderer—was nowhere to be seen.

The life jacket was already floating me upward toward the surface of the lake, and I kicked hard to help it. I needed air, and I didn't think I was going to make it.

A distant splash made me think of whales and how they slapped their tails on the water.

My eyes were bulging. My lungs were burning. I couldn't tell how far away the air was. I thought maybe, if I inhaled, it would be okay. The darkness was closing in around me.

A solid body kicked up behind me and grabbed the back of my vest. I rose faster with their help, and a moment later, my head breached the surface. I took a huge breath, followed by a series of coughs that racked my body.

"I've got you," Eli said next to my ear. He turned me onto my back in a lifeguard hold and swam us both to the boat's ladder.

Once we were back on the boat, I flopped onto the cushioned bench, stared at Eli, and asked, "Why did you push me?"

Eli's eyes widened. "I didn't—"

"I'm kidding," I said with a weak smile.

Eli melted and sat down on the bench beside me. "The life vest should've kept you afloat. Are you okay?"

"I'm okay. Don't apologize. It wasn't your fault. I told you. I'm cursed."

"I'll take you back." He left a trail of water as he went back to the helm and started the boat.

He showed no sign that he'd seen my attacker, and I decided not to mention it. The last thing I needed was a worried Eli hovering over me.

CHAPTER 15

MUSE *dreams of betrayal.*

S cratch was back, but he couldn't get to me, and I wasn't going out there again. My belly ached where he'd clawed me. The bite on my shoulder throbbed.

I was still wearing the collar that the evil vet had put on me, and I did *not* want Scratch to see me like that. I felt humiliated, and so I hid in the bedroom where the curtains were drawn.

I slept. I dreamt.

I was in my native form: humanoid feline. My legs were long, my muscles strong. I felt young and healthy. No aches, no pains.

I was seated upon my throne, in Whiskers—my kingdom. The forest surrounded us, white birch trees, wild and straight. Their branches arched over the clearing, dappling the golden sunlight that streamed down on us. Giant slices of stone covered the ground, carved with intricate swirls and flowers. The craftsfolk of Whiskers were renowned, and I admired the beauty they'd created.

My royal subjects surrounded me, begged to know where I'd been. Old, young, male, female, kittens...I knew all their faces. They loved me. And I loved them. Their whiskers and tails twitched with excitement, as did mine. I was happy. I was home.

The moment the dream turned sour, I sensed it. A shadow fell upon the court. The crowd parted from the middle outward, revealing a body lying prone on the stone, blood spreading into the carvings, swirls and flowers blooming red.

It was her. My beloved mate. And my guts wrenched at the sight.

Scratch loomed over her corpse. His robes blew around him, flicked about with the electric swish of his tail. Expression hard, he stabbed a finger at me. Accusing me.

"Murderer!"

The faces of my kin changed. They grew accusatory. Angry. My subjects hissed words of condemnation. They believed that I had done this deed.

They were not wrong. Though I had not dealt the death blow, my overconfidence had killed the one I loved more than life itself. I had underestimated my enemies.

"Murderer!"

I awoke with a start, sat up, and panted until my heart rate slowed.

I'm the Snuggleupagus!
— Diana (age 5) when she wanted a cuddle

◆

CHAPTER 16

DIANA *observes Jake Lamb.*

Chief Deputy Nick called me into work. He needed me for A/V support. On a Saturday. It annoyed me but also gave me something to do besides clean. After the poop fiasco, I was disenchanted with mopping.

The miner left shortly after I'd arrived. He'd gotten his message across and had gone off to watch a game, or hang with his kids, or do whatever creepers do when they're not being creepy. Nevertheless, I made sure to lock the door when I left to go to work.

I'd been riding my old bike back and forth. Mom needed the car. *Her* car. *The* courts had impounded my car along with *my* husband's other assets. I'd gotten used to it. There was one hill that was a beyotch going home, but the ride to work was easy enough. The wind on my face and the sun warming my back were refreshing.

The station was half-deserted—quiet day. Unless the moon was full, the Wyrdwood Sheriff's Department never stayed super busy. On weekends, most people didn't come in unless called in.

Walking down the hallway, I had a moment of high-school PTSD when my nemesis, Brenda Doill, came toward me from the opposite direction. Without warning, I was back at Wyrdwood North High School, on my way to math class.

I'd known Brenda since grade school, when she and I had been friends. I never figured out what made her turn evil, but somewhere in middle school—right around puberty—her eyes took on a red glow whenever she looked at me. My friends said she was jealous, but I didn't see how that could be true. She was prettier, smarter, and more coordinated than I had ever hoped to be.

As a nerdy high school student, I'd given her a wide berth. Whenever we passed in the halls, I'd clutched my books to my chest and kept my eyes downcast. I'd prayed she wouldn't notice me. For some reason, though, she always did. And her bully-fu was much stronger than my invisibility cloak. She'd flipped my books up out of my arms on many occasions. She thought it was hilarious.

To my astonishment, adulthood had softened her.

"Brenda," I said in greeting.

"Diana." She continued on past me.

I thought, *How civilized. How grown-up*. And I smiled to myself.

Then Brenda added, "Banana." Her childhood nickname for me had caused me many embarrassing moments in the school cafeteria. She'd started it when she noticed that my mother packed a banana in my lunchbox every day. *Diana Banana. Diana Banana*. The name-calling had escalated when, in sex ed, the teacher had used a banana to demonstrate how to put on a condom.

Too embarrassed to tell Mom, I started throwing the bananas away before the bell rang. Nevertheless, the mean nickname stuck.

And Brenda was doing her dang best to resurrect it.

To my credit, I did not respond. I was on a mission. I was needed. I was important. My boss, the most powerful and—if I may say so—hottest deputy in the building, had called me in to record an interview. I felt Brenda's gaze on the back of my head, but I ignored it.

I paused at my desk to drop off my backpack and jacket. I'd tidied the desktop before I left on Thursday, knowing I'd be OOF—out of office—on Friday, spelunking with Eagle. I had "regular hours"—airquotes intentional—but they were just a suggestion. The fact that they had called me in on a Saturday was evidence of that.

Nick was in his office with the door open. I knocked and poked my head in. "Hey."

He squinted up at me. "Took you long enough. What did you do? *Walk* here?"

I entered the office. "I'll have you know that I was busy helping orphans and puppies when you called. I abandoned them to be here. You should appreciate me more."

"I don't have to appreciate you. I pay you." Nick stood. "We've got a witness waiting to be interviewed. I need you to set up the equipment."

"Sure. Who is it?"

"Contessa Fekettay. You know her?"

"No."

"Her client's death was ruled an accident, but we need her statement on record. Crossing our Is and dotting our Ts."

He walked by me and out of the office. I followed. "The subject and her attorney are in B. Come find me when you're ready."

It took hardly any time to check the equipment. I'd set it up myself and done a darn good job. The recording device was on the other side of the wall from interview room B. A one-way mirror separated the two rooms. The device recorded two copies of the video feeds and the audio, one copy to the cloud and one to an SD memory card. It was overkill, but lives depended on them. *My job* depended on them.

I let Nick know he could begin, then returned to the observation room to monitor the recording device.

Beyond the mirror, two men stood against the wall behind a woman seated at a rectangular table. I had positioned two cameras in opposite corners, and the microphone was on the ceiling above the table.

Nick joined them.

One of the men—the handsome one—held himself like he was always in charge, professorial in corduroy pants and a serious button-down shirt. The other man was well over six and a half feet tall, slim as if he'd been stretched, old and scarred like an alley cat. The woman might have been a wrestler. She fidgeted in her seat and tapped her short nails on the tabletop. I didn't know who they were until Nick kicked off the interview by asking them to identify themselves.

They all had spark, though I couldn't tell which kin they came from. They veiled their magickal identities even to other kith.

The men pulled out chairs and sat.

The woman sought the approval of the man in corduroy pants. When he nodded, she said, "Tessa Fekettay." Her words came out staccato and alto, rebellious. She was not happy to be there. She had a rectangular body, muscular and thick. Her head was blocky with a square jaw and flat-top hairdo, shaved at the sides. She wore pronounced cat-eye makeup and had accentuated eyebrows, both of which flew in counterpoint to the masculinity of her clothes. A yellow genderless blazer exaggerated the breadth of her shoulders. Black pants and a plain black t-shirt downplayed her curves. She was the kind of person who could bench-press a hundred pounds then play a delicate flute solo and make you cry.

I didn't know what would happen, but I was rooting for her.

The tall man waited to be sure Tessa was done, then said, "Asger Jorgenson." He pronounced it 'AHS-gare YOR-gen-son.' It sounded a bit like he was clearing his throat.

Mr. Jorgenson towered over everyone, even seated. An older man, he had a natural slouch to his back, undoubtedly the result of bending to avoid chandeliers and low-flying planes.

His skin had a tough tan, the kind you get from being a welder or riding camels in the desert, bombarded by sand. One side of his face hung slack, unmoving, as if he'd had a stroke. He had a gnarly scar on that side, long-since hardened. The eye on the same side was the purple of irises or of royalty. The other, the one on his uninjured side, was the blue of a winter sky.

He wore an olive-colored dress-shirt tucked into canvas pants. He'd draped a navy and white windbreaker over his arm, and a brimmed hat covered the tips of his ears.

When the silence stretched too long, Nick said, "I need you

to do the same, please, Jake. State your name for the recording."

"Oh, sorry," said the man in corduroy pants. "I'm Jake Lamb of Lost Lambs Haven. As you know, Jorgi and I are here to provide Nurse Fekettay's alibi for the time of Harold Fishgiven's unfortunate death."

I sat up.

"All right," said Nick. "I'm listening. Where were you that day?"

Jake Lamb's and Nurse Fekettay's eyes met. Mr. Lamb spoke first. "Before we get into that, I'd like to ask a question. Are you thinking Mr. Fishgiven's death resulted from negligence? Is there a criminal investigation underway?"

Nick leaned forward, hands up in a soothing gesture. "No. We're covering all our bases before we put the case to bed. We've already concluded that it was an accident. We don't believe anyone was at fault."

"It makes sense. Tessa was with us on a hike in Willamette National Forest. We were meeting a client there. We left last Monday and got back this morning. On the way back, we heard you wanted to speak to Tessa. Sorry for the delay. We had no cell service where we were."

"No problem." Nick made a note on his laptop. "So, you work for the Lost Lambs Haven, is that correct?"

"Yes."

"How is it that you came to be caring for Mr. Fishgiven?"

"I moonlight. I put an ad in the Gazette, and Mrs. Fishgiven called me. He needed someone to help him in and out of bed. I agreed, though I warned them I'd be gone this past week. Lost Lambs comes first."

Jake Lamb smiled and nodded his approval.

Nick asked, "How long did you work for the Fishgivens?"

"Three weeks. I started the day he came home after his surgery. He was bedridden for the first week, had a catheter, and needed watching so he didn't throw a clot. I was there mornings then again in the late afternoons. In the second week, he was starting to get around with help. He had a walker."

"Was Mrs. Fishgiven there too?"

"Sometimes, yeah, but he still needed me."

"Why's that?"

"No way she could've taken care of him. Half the time, she couldn't even remember my name."

"What are you saying?"

"She's declining, you know? Up here." She indicated her temple. "Like a piano with a broken hammer. Sounds great until you hit that toneless key."

"You think she has dementia?"

"Meh. Lots of things can cause forgetfulness. I told her she should go see her doctor."

"Ms. Fekettay, do you remember seeing any home-canned food in Mr. Fishgiven's cabinets or refrigerator?"

"No." Tessa still had resistance in her tone, but she sounded sincere. "If I had, I'd have checked it. Decelerating patients, you know? Not always paying attention."

"So, it doesn't surprise you that Mr. Fishgiven's cause of death was botulism? Food poisoning?"

The caregiver pursed her lips and shook her head. "Food was his drug. He was always eating something."

A wave of dizziness overtook me. I swayed in my chair, and in the next second, I realized I wasn't the only one.

"Did you feel that?" Tessa asked, grabbing the edge of the table.

"Felt like a tremor," Jake Lamb said.

Nick puffed out some air. "Haven't had one of those in a while."

"No. We haven't." Something in Lamb's deadpan voice painted a layer of doom on his words.

Nick heard it too. He looked askance at Lamb before turning his attention back to Tessa and saying, "I think we're done here, Ms. Fekettay." Nick pushed back his chair and stood. "Thanks very much for coming in." He opened the door.

The others stood as well. Jake Lamb hung back to let the others leave before him. He put a hand on Nick's shoulder, revealing a large gold ring, and said, "It was a pleasure to see you again, Nick. Give my best to your dad."

Nick smiled. "I will, thanks."

I hurried to the recording-room door and opened it as Jake Lamb walked by in the hall. He was taller up-close-and-personal, and he smelled like pine.

"Hi," I said before I could stop myself.

He glanced at me, said, "Hi," and kept walking.

I smiled as if he'd given me a flower.

On the way back to my desk, I observed Brenda entering the restroom. I paused. A rare opportunity presented itself. I could be an angel, or I could be a devil. I decided that it couldn't hurt to explore the possibilities. I strolled over to Brenda's cubicle, to see what was what. The modular walls were only five feet high, so I crouched out of sight.

Spying on the enemy was a well-known tactic for survival. I hoped to gain insight into her character.

Brenda's desk was a Japanese anime circus. It had figurines of girls dressed in very skimpy outfits, some with tails and ears or horns, appearing ready to raise a storm—literally—or kick someone's butt—also literally.

Brenda had no magick whatsoever. No wonder she collected fantasy characters. I could imagine her doing cosplay as one of them.

I found myself softening to her, and that would never do. I shook myself. Brenda had bullied me throughout high school, and she seemed committed to continuing as an adult. She and I could never be friends.

My gaze drifted over Brenda's monitor, and I read a bit of what she'd been typing. It was a long letter to someone. The screen showed the second page, so I couldn't tell who the recipient was. She was laying her heart out, begging the person to reconsider their decision to leave Wyrdwood. I realized as I read that Brenda would go ballistic if she knew I'd seen it. She was vulnerable.

I hovered between two options: angel or devil? Which was I?

I typed control-A, selected the entire text, then hovered my finger over the delete key.

What would it hurt?

Maybe I'd be saving her from making a fool of herself. We've all written those desperate letters to boyfriends or girlfriends who just broke up with us. Been there. Done that.

What was the worst that could happen? She'd have to rewrite it, which meant she'd have the opportunity to rethink what she'd say.

I'd be doing her a favor.

I peered over the cubicle wall toward the bathroom. My finger twitched.

I didn't want to do Brenda any favors.

I pulled my hand back. Angel, then. Mom would be proud.

I turned to leave Brenda's cubicle, checking for witnesses.

Then, in my head, I heard her voice, *"Diana Banana."*

I stopped, turned around, and slammed the delete key.

Devil after all.

◆ ◆ ◆

CHAPTER 17

KITTY *snubs Bowtie.*

Eli said goodbye with a hug that lasted a second too long. He dropped me off on the Fishgiven dock and offered to accompany me to the house. I refused. I wanted to be alone.

I managed to cross Martha's house without getting lake water everywhere and went to the bathroom. After falling in, I was chilled to the bone. A hot shower revived me, and I breathed more than one sigh of relief standing under the soothing water.

The doorbell rang as I stepped out of the shower.

I wrapped myself in one of Martha's fluffy bathrobes.

The doorbell rang a second time.

I turbaned my head with a towel as I crossed the ballroom.

The doorbell rang again, this time with multiple insistent presses.

"Coming!"

I opened the door, and all I saw was...bowtie.

A beat of mutual shock passed between us, then he asked, "What are *you* doing here?" His tone held a sneer.

I returned the volley. "What are *you* doing here?"

He looked me up and down.

I did the same to him. Standing before me was the man who had cursed me. A bug-eyed lizard of a man, he had a knack for moving his eyes without moving the rest of him. He parted his dishwater-blond hair in the middle and slicked it back on both sides. His business suit was dark brown, his shirt green, and his bowtie was striped red, white, and purple. It did not match his suit, though it did match the snarly expression on his face.

When he didn't reply, I asked, "Are you stalking me?" I wondered where I'd set my phone, wishing I could film him.

"I'm not stalking you," he spat back at me. "I'm here to see Martha Fishgiven." His voice squeaked when he talked, and I heard him in my head shouting at me, "Your family will pay... Cursed! You are cursed!"

"Martha isn't here." I didn't think it was possible, but the man's expression puckered even tighter.

"Where is she?"

"In Europe, taking her husband's remains to be buried with his family. Would you like me to give her a message?"

The bowtied avenger sniffed hard enough that he almost sucked in his whole nose. "No." He turned on his heel and stormed off a few steps.

I was about to slam the door, when he halted and said, "Tell her to call the bank. We need to speak to her about the loan her husband cosigned. Ewan Trelor is unable to make payments. Soon, we'll be forced to start proceedings to collect on it." He didn't wait for a reply nor did he check to ensure I'd heard him. He just left, his spine stick-straight, and his jaw clenched.

"Her husband just died, jerk!" I shouted after him. He gave no indication that he'd heard me.

I knew his message related to the paperwork Martha wanted to find. At least, he hadn't reinforced the curse he'd placed on me and mine. He hadn't needed to. His curse had already almost killed me—three times.

Once I was dressed and had a hot mug of tea in hand, I phoned the one person I knew might help me with the curse: her highness, Mayor Violet Bagley.

"Kitty Kats, is it?" she said when the receptionist forwarded me to her office.

"Yes, Mayor."

"Please. It's Violet." Mayor Violet Bagley seemed about eighteen to me, although I knew her to be much older. She was petite and adorable, and she ruled Wyrdwood with an iron fist. Magickal in nature, she was also the law when it came to beings with the spark. The sheriff—a Normal—was ill-equipped to handle the sparky mischief in Wyrdwood. Good folk respected Mayor Violet, and bad folk feared her. Rightly so. Her form of justice made Normal justice look like a light scolding.

"Violet. Are you well?"

"I am. What is it you need, Mrs Kats? I'm a busy person."

"Call me Kitty, please. I was hoping you'd give me a referral to someone who deals with curses."

"Who's cursed?"

"Me."

"Who cursed you?"

I debated telling her, but that mean voice inside that thought I deserved to be cursed wouldn't let me. "It doesn't matter. I just need to get it removed."

"I see. Well, try calling Vicky Fort. She's a warlock. You'll find her in the town business directory. If she can fit you into her busy schedule, you'll be in capable hands."

"Thank you."

"Goodbye, Kitty. And good luck."

"Good—"

The mayor hung up.

I said the final word anyway. "Bye."

I looked up Vicky Fort and found Madam Victoria Fort in the directory.

A robotic voice answered the call.

"Fort Salon," he said. "Tell me your trouble in as few words as possible."

"I'm cursed, and I'd like it removed."

"Your name?"

"Kitty Kats."

"Is the curse familial or personal?"

"I'm not sure."

"Come tomorrow morning at nine o'clock sharp. I will text you the expected fee and the address."

"Um, do you think—"

The man hung up.

"Well, okay then. Apparently, everyone is busier than I am."

A second later, as if he'd had it queued, the text message popped up.

I immediately felt buyer's remorse about making an appointment with a warlock.

I spent time playing with Martha's kitties. They had a wand toy that they chased. It didn't take them long to get tired, and I found myself playing alone. My mind wandered back to the curse, the warlock, and my debt.

"My life is poo, kitties. The mortgage is paid for now, but I'll be out of money again soon. Diana's trying, but she's got her own problems. Thing is, I never once thought my husband could die. One day, he was there. Next day, he wasn't. Poof. Just like that."

Faffy and Smaug were watching me. They were attentive listeners.

To avoid working myself into a fretting frenzy, I did a deep clean on the litter boxes. No matter how prissy the cat, they always manage to get the sides of the box dirty. Bleach wipes come in handy for that.

Needing more to occupy my mind, I returned to Harold's

office to continue what I'd started that morning. I stood over his desk and my attention landed on the note from Rhiannon. The break-up note. I pulled it out of the box and examined it.

How long ago had they broken up? It couldn't have been long. The paper showed no sign of age, despite its crumpled state. When I sniffed it, the faint smell of lake water came off it. It was handmade, the edges rough and texture au naturel. It mentioned the new moon.

The previous night, I'd seen a waxing crescent moon in the sky.

I pulled out my phone again and did research, feeling smarter than I looked.

The night Harold died, there was a new moon in the sky.

◆ ◆ ◆

CHAPTER 18

DIANA *and Eagle join forces.*

The regret kicked in before I'd even made it to my desk. All that pent-up anger from years of being Brenda's target had poured into my index finger as I'd pressed that Delete key.

Maybe it wasn't too late. I could go back and do a CTRL-Z. Bring her document back. She'd never know. My stomach churned. I wasn't that person.

Turning on my heel, I started to go back.

Brenda came out of the bathroom.

I ducked behind a pillar. Options formed in my mind. I could 'fess up and tell her how to bring it back. I could return to my desk and stew in my guilt. Or, I could watch her reaction.

I hovered on the edge of indecision.

Brenda strode toward her cubicle, pulled out her chair, and

sat down out of sight.

I had to wend my way through the hive to where I could see her again.

She was staring at the empty page. Her head slumped, and she cradled it with her hands over her eyes.

A coworker walked by me, and I pretended to be busy. We shared a smile and a nod. Then, I went back to watching.

Brenda was looking around the room.

I bent behind a cubicle wall in the nick of time. Or so I thought. I held my breath and backed away.

My butt ran into something—or rather someone—firm. I didn't dare look.

"What you doin'?" a familiar voice asked. Eagle.

I stood up tall and faced him. A glance over my shoulder told me Brenda was fixated on her monitor, not me. I turned his question around on him. "What are *you* doing? I thought we agreed you would call and not show up unannounced at my job. Come with me." I turned him around and pushed him toward my desk.

"Who're you spying on?"

Defensive, I raised my voice higher than I intended. "I wasn't spying on anyone."

One side of Eagle's mouth tucked up. "Then what was up?"

"Nunya."

"Nunya?"

"Nunya business."

We had arrived at my desk by the window. I wasn't in a cubicle like most of my coworkers. I preferred a window seat.

The sunshine flowed in and reflected off the silver web of a thousand paper clips. I have a bin of them on my desk, or I *used* to have a bin of them. Someone had not just overturned the bin, they had poured the paperclips all over my desk, my chair, and the floor under my desk. Brenda.

I smiled, not feeling as guilty about *my* prank. She had to have done it before she went to the bathroom, before my internal devil had even suggested that I invade her space.

"Wow," Eagle commented. "Looks like you got an enemy."

Truer words were never spoken.

I began swiping the paperclips off the desktop and into my palm. "Why are you here, Eagle?" I sounded more irritated than I intended.

Eagle glanced around before answering. "I gotta do another stakeout. The miners. Thought you might wanna come."

I stood up straighter and faced him, holding a handful of the clips. I wasn't sure how I wanted to answer. My initial reaction wasn't just 'No,' it was 'Hell no.' But my second reaction held more curiosity. "Why?"

"My boss wants to know more about these miners, how the op works. Their buyer. We don't have to go through the Birth Canal again."

"The Birth Canal?"

"Y'know. That tunnel you got stuck in."

"It has a name?"

"Common knowledge." Eagle gave me a crooked smile. Damn him.

I gave him a suspicious look. "Isn't it too late to get in there before they arrive?"

"We're going to follow the head guy when he leaves. See where he goes."

"It's the weekend. You sure they'll be there?"

"They're there. I drove by on my way here. So, you in?"

I admit that I enjoyed the stakeouts with Eagle. I felt safe with him. Illogical, I know.

I also liked that Eagle didn't talk much, and he didn't complain that *I did*. Besides, he was easy on the eyes, and light flirting did me good. It reminded me I was a soon-to-be-divorced hottie. I viewed it as my training wheels.

Nevertheless, I hesitated. I said, "There's something I have to tell you."

"And?"

"He came to my house."

"Who did?"

"That Herne. The head guy. He was parked on my street, waiting for me."

"What'd he say?"

"Nothing. He just wanted me to know that he knew where I lived."

A dark cloud spread over Eagle's face. "All right," he said, and the muscle in his cheek clenched. "I'm not putting you in danger. I'll go alone. Thanks, anyway." He started to turn away, but I put a hand on his forearm.

The moment he decided to leave me out of it, I wanted in. "You can't go by yourself," I said.

"Why not?"

"It's dangerous. What if something happened?"

"Nothing's gonna happen."

I narrowed my eyes. "Friends don't let friends spelunk alone, even if they're not in a cave. I'm coming with you. No mangy buck with an attitude is going to scare me away." I poked him in one hard pec. "I'm ready to get out of here anyway." I glanced toward Brenda, only to catch her eye.

She was watching me. She had the nerve to bounce her eyebrows at me.

"Let's go," I said to Eagle. "I rode my bike today. You can pick me up at my place in an hour. I need to change."

"You sure?"

"I'm sure."

"All right, then. Wear black. Something with a hood."

"You're in charge of snacks." I grabbed my backpack and bike helmet, and I turned away from the paperclip mess. That was a project for Tomorrow Diana.

CHAPTER 19

MUSE *visits an old ally.*

Greta had fallen asleep next to me. Her nearness warmed me, but it also made the skin on my back prickle and jump. I had to get up. You can only take so much of a good thing before it strangles you.

I was still shackled by the giant plastic collar—and I had an itch. An itch! An itch that I couldn't scratch. I rolled and rubbed, trying to rid myself of the collar. Who does that to someone? It's my body! If I want to lick it or scratch it or show it off, I am well within my rights.

Over the next five minutes, freedom became an obsession. I had to get the collar off. I lay on my back and kicked at it. I scraped it against a table leg. I tried to bite it. I knew I looked ridiculous, and when I saw Mini-Mimi watching with that smirk on her face, I lost it. I channeled my frustration into an epic hiss directed at her.

She skedaddled.

In one last-ditch effort, I forced the collar through the doorway into the litter cabinet, snagged it there, then backed up, pulling my head out as I went. I scraped an ear, but I'm a genius. I left the collar where it belonged, with the poop.

Free, my first thought was food. I ate like a cat reborn then found a ray of sunshine in which to meditate. My life had grown complicated in recent days, but I hadn't forgotten my prime directive: survival. The logic was obvious. In order to survive, I needed to avoid Scratch until I'd healed, and I needed Kitty to survive so she could attend to my needs. I had no delusions about the fact that Diana would drop me at the nearest animal prison the moment Kitty was dead.

All that talk about Ladies of the Lake had me worried. I'd known they were in the area, but they kept to themselves. Kitty had seen one, and that was a dark enough omen that it twitched my whiskers. I knew general things, but I needed more information if I was going to keep Kitty safe.

There's only one cat who knows more than I do. We call him Old Tom, and he lives in the interstitial layer between Wyrdwood and my kingdom.

Once upon a time, Tom was my royal advisor. When they exiled me, he chose to leave as well, though he refuses to live in Reality with me. He's set in his ways and prefers to surround himself with as much magick as possible. I've always suspected that it kept him from dying of old age. Unlike me, Old Tom is not immortal.

In order to visit Old Tom, I had to get out of the house. Then, I had to get past my nemesis unseen. Nothing is ever easy! Silver lining—as I said before, I'm a genius.

Kitty's bedroom window was open. I sprung onto the bed with grace, careful not to strain my wound. From there, only a screen separated me from the great outdoors. I made short work of it, clawing a hole large enough for me to slip through. Kitty would have a hissy-fit when she saw it, but that wasn't my problem. I had bigger fish to fry.

I slunk from the bush to tree trunk, to garbage can, to the gap under the fence where I could crawl into the neighbor's yard. No sign of Scratch. He was undoubtedly still staring daggers at the front of the house.

The best way to reach Old Tom was to call him from Rotgut Alley. I sniffed around to find any sign of him, but the alley's stank was nose-blinding. I bounded to the top of a dumpster from where I had a clear view in both directions of the alley. I didn't want any surprises.

I let out my first yowl of summoning—that of a cat in heat. Every subsequent yowl was identical, and I spaced them apart with practiced regularity.

The wind blew bits of paper and dry leaves along the cobblestones. Shadows consolidated and darkened. The clouds slid by overhead. Every resident on the alley shouted at me to shut up.

Time passed.

My voice was getting hoarse, and still Old Tom hadn't shown. I worried he'd expired and no one had bothered to tell me. The sun dipped low, and the alley grew chilly.

Just as I thought longingly about dinner, there was a pop like a balloon exploding. Old Tom appeared beside the dumpster, took a couple steps, then sat and blinked with slow deliberation.

"King Muse," he said, his voice familiar and beloved.

"Ol' Tom, you ol' dog." I dropped down to sit with him. I slow-blinked back at him, signaling my respect. I had more whiskers than friends to whom I'd slow-blink. "How've you been keeping yourself?" He had lost weight, and his Siamese markings appeared darker than before. His age was catching up with him. It had been years since I'd last seen him.

"Well, sire. Well. And you?"

"Well enough. Any news from the kingdom?"

Old Tom shook his head. "Nothing." He was usually my source of information on the kingdom. He spoke to everyone.

"It's been a long time since you last had news."

"True, sire. They have perhaps closed the kingdom to visitors. Isolated themselves."

"Mm. Fools."

I caught Old Tom staring at my shaved fur and wound, and I felt the need to explain. "It's nothing," I said. "Just a nick, given to me by Scratch. He's back."

"Ah. I presume you gave him worse?"

"Of course. He never learns his lesson."

"Is that why you've sought me out?"

"No. I need your knowledge of local history. Something is happening in Wyrdwood, and it has my scruff afluff."

Old Tom narrowed his eyes then stood. "Let's get out of here so we can speak freely." He turned his back on me and lifted the end of his tail. "Latch on."

I followed the tail's slow undulation, gauging its timing, then—at the exact right moment—I caught it in my mouth. It tasted of dust and old cat. I held it gently and waited.

I could not enter the Interstice on my own. It's a function of my exile. For this reason, I had to piggyback on Old Tom's magick.

My guide took three steps forward, and I went along with him, like a dog on a leash. I hoped no one saw me.

A wave of fog engulfed us, erasing first the hard edges, then everything. I perked my ears, turning them this way and that as the sounds of Wyrdwood—the cars, the voices, the wind, water, airplanes, trees, footfalls, and birds—faded into silence. The aromas of Reality withdrew to be replaced by the dry nothingness of the Interstice.

The Interstice is a buffer. It keeps strata from bumping into one another or overlapping. Anyone who travels between realms, passes—briefly and perhaps unknowingly—through the Interstice. A rare few have managed to carve out a home there.

I've never understood why Old Tom chooses to live in the gap. I've asked him many times, and I always get the same answer, "Because here, the possibilities are endless." I used to think that meant he liked it because he could flee into many other realms, but in recent decades, I've concluded that he enjoys the existential, noncommittal emptiness of it.

To each their own. Me, I find it unnerving. There are no trees, no buildings, no sky—and anyone you meet there could be anything from any dimension or pocket realm. The ground I feel beneath my feet is nothing but a memory. Gravity is an illusion created by my own mind to keep me oriented.

Most *sane* inter-realm travelers pass through the Interstice without stopping, 'chuting on to their destination. The Interstice has no inherent rules imposed by either local physics or socio-political beliefs. In the Interstice, we revert to our natural forms—the form into which we were born in our home realms. For me, I take on the resplendent form I once had in my kingdom.

The Interstice has a never-changing ambient temperature— neither hot nor cold—so I was just as comfortable without my fur as I had been with it. An outsider would have seen two naked humanoid men, one old and wrinkled, one quite handsome. I say "humanoid" because in the Interstice, the top of my head remains cat-like, with elegant cat ears and the same gorgeous eyes. From the eyes down, I am humanoid and able to speak like they do. I have sexy masculine lips. I'm impressive. And yet, I am not human.

I can only revert to my native form while in the Interstice. I presume because interstitial magick overpowers the curse placed upon me by my enemies when I was exiled. In every other realm, I am doomed to be an adorable tuxedo cat with an exceptionally impressive tail.

My enemies thought they were punishing me by locking me in cat form, but I have come to identify as 'cat,' and I prefer that lifestyle. I am a cat. I am a king. It matters not what physical form I take.

Old Tom's tail disappeared the moment we entered the space between worlds. I licked the taste of him away and plucked a hair from my tongue with my fingers. Old Tom stood up onto his two legs, towering over me. He resembled a scrawny baby bird before the feathers come in. Seeing him wrinkled and sagging with age, a wild shock of white hair on his head, I felt a surge of affection mingled with sadness. He had aged. I had not thought that possible, and I wondered if he saw a difference in me, too.

I got to my feet, wobbling and weak. It had been so long since I'd been in my native form that I felt imbalanced, a fact that I did my best to hide from Old Tom.

To his credit, he turned his back so as not to embarrass me.

Once I felt stable on my feet and could walk forward to join him, Old Tom said, "This way," and he led me into the white nothingness. I stayed near him, though I trusted he would find me if I strayed.

"Here." Old Tom stopped in a place that was no different from the spot where we entered. "If you so desire, we can sit."

I sat cross-legged. The ground had softened and was quite comfortable. A warm breeze blew across my back.

Old Tom sat facing me. "Sire, I'm glad you sought me out. I was about to come looking for you. The Reality realm is on the verge of great catastrophe."

My old friend was known to use poetic phrasing from time to time, but his expression told me he wasn't just making conversation. "Go on," I prompted him.

"First, sire, if you don't mind, I'd like to know why you came. What is happening?" He folded wrinkled hands in his lap.

"Of course, I have missed you, Tom. So, I pounced at any excuse to visit."

"You don't need an excuse, sire. But in this case, what is it?"

"A Lady of the Lake recently came ashore. My chatelaine encountered one. I'm not sure what it means, but I'm inclined to protect her—Kitty, my chatelaine, I mean. Not the wretched Lady of the Lake. I'm hoping to learn about the creatures that live in the waters of Talyllyn."

"I see. The Ladies are very powerful. I suggest you avoid them. You do not want to get involved in coming events."

"What do you know?" I narrowed my eyes and tilted my chin. Old Tom had my attention.

"One hears things, sire, here in the Interstice. You remember the giant under the mountain?"

I nodded. "I assume it sleeps there still?"

"Yes, and it has slept soundly ever since Wyrdwood made its journey from the old country to the Oregon Territory. The same shielding wards that protect you also guard the giant. It is the well of magick that fuels Wyrdwood. The Fates keep him asleep."

"I'm aware."

"What you may not know is that the giant has been stirring. There are those who strive to awaken it."

"Why?"

"Because when the giant wakes, it will destroy Reality."

"I don't understand. Who would want that?"

"Kith who want to retake Reality. To do that, they must cow or kill all Normals. They intend to use the giant as their first volley."

"I see."

"The idiots don't understand the consequences of their actions. They've been performing ceremonies and sacrifices to rouse it."

"Poking the proverbial bear."

"Yes, sire. A bear imbued with godlike power and as much emotional intelligence as a toddler."

"I doubt there's anything I can do to prevent this."

"Heroic as you are...no. There are others working to counter it, though I'm not sure they understand the magnitude of what they're fighting."

"If only I had the means to communicate with Reality's inhabitants."

"I know, sire."

"Is there *nothing* I can do?"

"You must also be ready, sire, in the event that you have to flee. I have something to give you." Old Tom held out his fist. An item appeared, clutched in his hand. It solidified. It was a torc, an ancient collar made of heavy braided silver. Nearly a full circle, the ends were capped with silver cat heads. I could feel its magick without even touching it.

"What's that for?" I leaned nearer to examine the delicate workmanship. The cats' eyes were slivers of amber.

"This will allow you and anyone you're touching to cross into the Interstice." He held the torc out to me. "Wear it at all times, if you please. You never know when the giant will rise."

"Thank you, Tom. This is a gift worthy of a king. I see and appreciate you."

Old Tom bowed forward, and I rested a long-fingered hand on his shoulder. I felt the touch of skin on skin all the way to my heart.

With a sniff, Old Tom shook off his emotion and sat up again.

To get back to business, I asked, "How are the Ladies of the Lake involved? Are they among those attempting to wake the giant?"

"Tch. They have too much to lose."

"Why would one come ashore?"

"For millennia, they have procreated with Wyrdwood's men."

"So?"

"The Talyllyn Ladies are an interesting species. All female, of course. They seduce husbands from other kin and breed with them."

"Rape?"

"No, no. The husband enters into a contract by choice. The Lady takes this commitment seriously, and in exchange for being given children, she offers magick in return. The husband is guaranteed a good life for as long as the marriage vow remains unbroken. A traditional contract requires a monthly rendezvous between the husband and the Lady until conception. This resumes a short time after the child's birth. Meanwhile, the husband lives a normal life on land. It's not a 'marriage' in the usual sense of the word. It's an exchange. The Lady gets children. The male gets lucky. No pun intended."

I smiled with amusement. "Interesting. So, a Lady surfaces once a month to have sex with her husband?"

"Yes. That's the primary reason they do. They tend to emerge during the new moon when it's darkest."

"This was broad daylight."

"That's odd. There must have been extraordinary circumstances."

"Like the death of her husband?"

"Perhaps, sire."

Old Tom and I visited for a while, reminiscing about my kingdom. He waxed nostalgic about my court, the courtiers, and how I ruled. I let him. Those were the good old days.

When the time came to go, I didn't dilly-dally. Goodbyes are never long with me. I used the torc to return to Reality, and it worked like a charm. Pun intended. I even managed to 'chute right to my neighborhood.

The sun was just coming up. I was so entrenched in thoughts of giants and lake-dwelling baby-mamas that I almost forgot to hide from Scratch. Lucky for me, he was stretched out on a tree branch, snoozing. I spotted him and ducked under a bush.

So, he had survived my assault. It had been centuries since we'd tangled. Why was he there? What did he want? I'd been so intent on kicking his ass that I hadn't bothered to ask. For the first time, it occurred to me that—perhaps—I should have.

No one had closed the window at the back, and I slipped inside undetected. The moment I set foot on the wood floor, I sensed that the energy inside the house had changed.

◆ ◆ ◆

No trouble too small. No curse too big.
Call 1-555-WARLOCK
—Wyrdwood Gazette classifieds

◆

CHAPTER 20

KITTY *gets treated.*

The warlock didn't fit any of my preconceived notions. I arrived early at the address, so I sat in my car, observing.

The house was a split-level, built in the 70s. Emerald-green shutters complemented white siding. Someone kept the lawn mowed, and an assortment of toys littered the front. A free-standing basketball hoop loomed by the curb.

Kids did Sunday-morning things up and down the street, riding bikes, playing kickball, and digging in the dirt. Their shouts and screams were a familiar percussive chorus.

The warlock's family had a silver SUV that had seen better days.

I evaluated what I was seeing and concluded that the warlock lived a middle-class life and had upwards of three children. I let out a relieved breath.

Then, a woman whispered in my ear, "You may come to the door when you're ready, Mrs. Kats."

I jerked around in my seat, but no one was there. I stared at the house and caught movement out of the corner of my eye.

A split second before it hit, I saw the baseball arcing toward my face. It slammed into the windshield and would have continued on through to my nose if the glass hadn't been laminated. As it was, the hard ball blasted the windshield into a spiderweb of shimmering cracks.

I leapt out of my skin.

A ginger girl came running out of a side yard, grabbed the ball, shouted, "Sorry," then hustled back to her game.

I moved in slow motion, turning my head to watch her go. My mind needed a moment to catch up. I triple-checked my mirrors before opening the car door.

I swore that if I made it through the day alive, I'd become a better person.

Madam Victoria Fort opened the door before I had a chance to ring the bell. My gaze traveled up to her face, taking in her wide-legged trousers—belted and pressed—and her starched masculine shirt. Her hair had once been all reddish brown before the gray infiltrated at her temples. She wore it in a messy bun at the back of her head, purposeful tendrils escaping in front to curl around her face. She stood at least six feet tall and was sturdier than she was voluptuous. Her features mirrored the chiseled, well-put-together style of her clothing. With her plain eyes and high cheekbones, she had an old-world beauty that made me feel small and dumpy. She wore no make-up. She didn't need any.

I think I was staring, because after a moment, she smiled with indulgence and said, "Mrs. Kats, I presume." It was the same voice I'd heard in the car, in my ear.

"Yes. I'm sorry. You're—"

"Victoria. It's a pleasure." She took a step back to open the door all the way and invited me in with a sweep of her arm. "We'll be going downstairs for your consultation."

I entered the foyer with a few dainty steps. One set of stairs ran up to the first floor, and another descended into the basement. I wasn't sure if she intended me to go on down, so I tucked myself to the side and waited for her while she locked the door.

"How many kids do you have?" I asked, attempting small talk.

"None."

"But, all the toys... the basketball hoop?"

"Smoke screen." Victoria smiled. "I give them to the neighbor kids in exchange for their eyes and ears."

My mouth dropped open.

"Not literally, of course." She added, a glint of humor in her smile. "They make excellent first-warning systems, though. When you're Normal and a warlock, every sparky, penis-bearing magick-wielder wants to test your mettle. I don't want my challengers showing up at my home."

"You're Normal?"

"Quite. You don't need magickal blood to wield magick, if you have the right tools. I tell you this because you appear female and thus are unlikely to challenge me to a pissing contest. Plus, I can see that you haven't come into your full spark yet. It's only just begun?"

I blinked. "That's right. How did you—"

Victoria tapped herself in the middle of her chest. "Warlock. Your equations are in the initial stages of expansion."

"My equations?"

"Shall we?" Victoria led the way down the stairs. She pushed open a door at the bottom. The smell of sage wafted out.

I covered the cough that arose from my throat. Heavy scents had always bothered me. When I was a kid, people said I had the nose of a cat.

Stark light illuminated every corner. Not a single shadow survived. Under normal circumstances, I would have expected the split-level's basement to hold a family room—a nest of warm browns and mismatched furniture. Victoria's space, however, was cold and stark. The lack of decor overturned my expectations.

Everything was white: the floor, the walls, and the lighting. Smooth linoleum covered the floor and had no scuffs on it. The low ceiling was a featureless expanse broken only by a grid of recessed lights.

The furniture comprised a stainless-steel embalming table, an easel with a two-foot square pad of paper on it, and a rolling doctor's stool in the center of the room. That was all.

I folded my hands together in front of my stomach to keep them from shaking.

"It is my understanding," said Victoria, "that you believe yourself to be cursed. Is that correct?"

"Yes." I had to clear my throat when my voice died. With feigned confidence, I repeated, "Yes. Um, before we get started, can I ask you something?"

"Very well."

"Are you familiar with the Talyllyn Ladies of the Lake?"

Victoria peered down her nose at me. "In an academic way. Are you having trouble with one?"

I shook my head. "Not me. I met one. She was married to a friend who passed recently. I suspect she may have been involved in his death."

"Murder?" Victoria leaned a hip against the steel table. "I've read about that kin. They live by a strict set of laws. They contract with a man to father their children. The man provides his sperm. The woman gives him her protection in the form of luck. The terms of the contract involve a regularly scheduled rendezvous during which they fornicate. These arrangements can last a lifetime. If the man fails to uphold the terms, he breaks the contract, and she withdraws her protection."

"She did that," I said, taking a step forward. "She removed his protection because he stood her up three times."

"Three is a powerful number."

"And that night, he was murdered."

"Hm. I'd say his luck ran out in a big way." Victoria patted the stool, indicating I should sit. "Now, let's start by confirming that you are indeed cursed. I can perhaps see what you're dealing with."

The stool was soft, well-padded, but a tad too high. Getting up onto it proved a bit awkward. Each time I tried to land a butt cheek, it rolled out of reach. Out of desperation, I pushed it against the table, so it couldn't roll, and managed to hop up.

While I'd been wrestling with the stool, Victoria had said nothing. Once I had successfully perched, she came to me. "Hang on." Then she rolled me away from the stainless-steel table. I became an island in a vast sea of insecurity.

"How much do you know about warlocks?" she asked.

"Not much. You're like witches, right?"

"Sort of. Many people believe that witches can only be female and warlocks can only be men. While I admit that witchcraft attracts far more female practitioners, and a majority of warlocks are men, gender is not what differentiates the two disciplines.

"Our tools differ from theirs. Witches use natural materials like moonlight, the elements, and eye of newt to work their magick. Warlocks use physics and the building materials of the cosmos. The language of warlock magick is mathematics." With that, she reached out and flipped a switch on the wall. The lights went out and, for a moment, we were cast into utter darkness.

I gasped aloud.

She flipped another switch. Black light exploded onto the room, painting anything white an electric blue and illuminating a chaotic—to me, at least—mural of numbers, letters, shapes, and symbols all over the walls, floor, and ceiling. I'd walked into a rave at the college of Mathematics. Except Victoria didn't seem ready to party at all.

Her blouse contrasted with everything else, glowing. It was, however, her skin that held my interest. She had markings all over her, geometric shapes arranged like a path that curled around her fingers, hands, and wrists; her neck; and her face. The whites of her eyes stood out, surrounding irises that had become black holes. When she spoke, her teeth glowed in a manner that made me uneasy.

"Relax," she said. "You're in no danger here. As long as you stay on that stool, you're anchored and safe. There are handles under the seat. You may want to grab hold."

She used her index finger to write something in the air, and the floor became transparent. It revealed a galaxy of stars and empty space below me.

I fumbled for the handles, anxiety rising.

She came up beside me, walking across the invisible floor. "Shhhh. You're twisting your vertices. Just relax." She put her hand on my shoulder, and a cascade of relaxation flowed through my entire body from that point.

"Listen for the plasma waves. Focus on them."

I heard nothing, at first. But I listened. A persistent hum emerged from the silence, and my body rocked in time with its ebb and flow.

Victoria nodded in approval then went to stand in front of the large pad of paper on the easel. She picked up some kind of wand and held it like one would a marker.

For the next thirty minutes, she drew on the pad in sporadic bursts, alternating between studying me and drawing. I couldn't see what she was doing since the pad had its back to me. I was a painter's model, posing as the master created my portrait. A couple times, she tore off a sheet and tossed it aside without ceremony.

She muttered numbers and words to herself that I couldn't quite hear.

As time passed, I slipped into a meditative state. I was aware, but relaxed and still. Stable. On any other day, sitting on a stool for that long would have made my back ache, but my spine felt straight and light, almost as if my flesh floated around it. The plasma waves flowed through me instead of bouncing off me.

Energetic tingles ignited in my limbs, my neck, and my scalp.

I realized that my breath had become slow, full, and easy.

I lost track of time.

I expanded and became one with the cosmos. The Earth rose to greet me. It hovered in front of me, a perfect, living ball. I could feel the energy streaming around and from it. The poles hooked the energy and kept it from flying off into space. Tiny, tiny beings ebbed and flowed across the surface. Enormous beings embraced the planet and rode the rivers of energy. They were indescribable. Gods. Monsters. Giants. They had neither bodies nor faces. Those were trivial things to them. They were before, above, and beyond time and space. They paid me no mind.

"Mrs Kats," came a voice from the other side of the universe. My dream snapped away. I heard, "Close your eyes."

Victoria flicked the light switch off and on. A wash of pink filtered through my eyelids.

"Flutter them open," she advised. "Let them get used to the light."

Her footsteps carried her back to the stand with the pad of paper, and she tore off the final sheet.

When I could see again, the room appeared as it had been when I first arrived. Small. Enclosed. Barren.

I realized I had long-since let go of the stool's handles.

Victoria took the sheet to the stainless steel table and jumped up to sit on it. "You're right," she said. "You're cursed."

I folded my hands in my lap, relaxed. "Can you help me?"

"I can't remove it. The curse is intrinsic."

"What does that mean?"

"It means you're the only one who can subtract it completely. You've introduced a fallacy that is throwing off your Aristotelian center of mass. Initially imposed on you by an external force, your current state incorporated it. Rather like a cancer. Your expression is turning on itself for some reason."

Her meaning hovered just beyond my grasp. "I don't understand. Can you say that in layman's terms?"

"Whatever you think caused the curse triggered something in your own psyche that is attracting negative experiences."

I grabbed the stool's handles again. "More layman than *that?*" I understood where she was going. I just didn't want to.

She studied me with clinical interest untarnished by sympathy. "The curse is self-imposed, Mrs. Kats. You're doing it to yourself."

"No," I said, shaking my head. "No, that's not it."

The warlock stared at me.

I broke the silence. "So, are you saying there's nothing you can do? I'm doomed?" I heard the sarcasm in that last question, and so did she.

"There is one thing I can do," she said with caution.

"Yes?"

"The fallacy that I mentioned, the one that has made you insoluble, has not yet taken root. I can subtract it from you, if you'd like. Return you to true."

Victoria Fort needed to work on her bedside manner.

I sifted out what she meant. "So, you can fix *me,* but not remove the curse. That's what you're saying?"

She nodded. "'Fixing you' will end the curse."

Exhaustion landed on me like a falling piano. "Maybe next time," I said.

Victoria nodded and hopped off the table. She gathered all the sheets of paper and folded them into quarters. She handed the pile to me. Instead of saying, 'These are yours,' she said, "These are you."

She steadied me while I slid off the stool.

"As to payment for my services," she said. "I won't charge you full price, since I was unable to do more than confirm the curse's existence. You may pay me in one of two ways. Either monetary compensation—half of our prearranged price—or you can owe me a favor."

"What kind of favor?"

"I don't know yet. It would be open-ended, but I promise you I am fair and honest. I won't ask more of you than matches the service I provided."

I felt a sense of connection to her that wasn't there when I'd entered her home. The session had given me that. In addition, her business tone and sincere expression made me trust her. I nodded. "If it's okay with you, the favor would be better for me. I'm in a bit of a tight spot financially."

"Yes, I know. Agreed. When I need your help, I will text you."

I walked to my car in a fog. The moment I pulled the door

shut, a deluge of feelings overwhelmed me. I broke into sobs. I couldn't control it. The last time I'd cried so hard, I was a child. I'd been in a car with my mother, and we got T-boned by another car. I wasn't hurt, not physically, but the emotional trauma was more than I could bear. In the aftermath of that accident, I'd cried almost as hard.

Once I'd calmed, I thought maybe I was overwhelmed by the vastness of the universe. Or maybe I was grieving the loss of that sense of peace I'd felt in Madam Victoria Fort's care.

◆ ◆ ◆

CHAPTER 21

DIANA *botches a stakeout.*

The sun was coming up. Eagle and I had been on stakeout at Hunter Herne's place, all night long. I was stiff, hungry, and grumpy.

We'd been sitting in silence for a while, and once or twice, I assumed Eagle had fallen asleep. Whenever I checked, however, his eyes were shiny slits that moved to one side to look back at me. Ever vigilant.

I gazed out the window and thought of my dad. It made my blood hot. I was still so livid. He'd died and left a colossal mess for my mom to clean up. He hadn't even bothered to get a respectable life insurance plan. I suspected I knew only a small percentage of the trouble he'd heaped on her. Mom was not a complainer. She bottled up her emotions and did what needed doing. Typical Mom.

If I was being honest, I wanted to strangle *her* too. She should've asked for help. If I hadn't moved in with her, I never would've found out about her debt. When I came across the bills and I realized what she'd been going through, my heart wrenched. Mom and I have had our problems—like all mothers and daughters, I suppose. But I love her. And I hated my dad. No. I didn't hate him. I was just furious with his dead ass.

"Hey," said Eagle, voice soft.

"What?"

"Stop digging your fingernails into my upholstery."

I opened my clenched fists. "Sorry."

"You hangry?" Eagle was watching me, no emotion on his face.

"Thinking of my dad."

"Ah."

"He died."

"Yeah."

"And left Mom saddled with debt."

"Kinda like your husband did to you."

"Yeah. I wish *he* were dead instead."

"Uh huh."

The notion of breakfast made me salivate. "Waffles. I need waffles. I deserve waffles."

"We're almost done here."

"Almost? Remind me what we're hoping to see?"

"The same as the past ten times you asked. We need to find out who these miners are working for."

"Right. Catch them delivering their take or something. Because it makes sense they'd do that at five o'clock on a Sunday morning." My sarcasm was ripe.

"That's when *I* would do it." Eagle sat up, pulling his seat-back upright with him. He'd been half-lounging.

Feeling restless, I gathered up the trash and put it into a plastic grocery bag. I swung around in the bucket seat and reached into the backseat to grab the empty soda bottles, coffee cups, and chip bags. Thus it was that the knock came on my door window just as I pressed my butt to it.

I spun around and dropped into my seat.

Hunter Herne IV was standing there, frowning in at me. He indicated I should lower my window.

I smiled and spoke so only Eagle could hear me. "We suck

at this."

Eagle started the car and pressed the button that rolled down the window.

Herne put his big man-hands on the frame and leaned down. "Mornin', Kats," he said. "What'cha doin'?"

"Nothin'." The word flew out of my mouth before I could stop it. The exchange had been our thing in high school. We'd pass in the hall, and he say, "Mornin', Kats. What'cha doin'?" And I'd reply "Nothin'." We'd smile and, all the while, I was squeeing inside that the cute boy knew my name. All that ended when he got what he wanted and moved on to the next girl. The fact that he remembered flabbergasted me.

Herne wasn't smiling. He wanted me to know that he knew who I was. In his native form, the one he worked so diligently to veil, his face was thinner and chin longer; and his cheekbones were beyond impressive. The antlers on his head had started to regrow. The new nubs were rounded and covered with velvety fur. I realized he hadn't *cut* them off, he'd shed them. When he pulled his lips back in a sneer, his teeth were thick and hard.

The only squee happening inside me was one of fear. His coffee breath reminded me of breakfast again. I hoped he wouldn't kill me before I could have waffles.

Hunter Herne snapped his fingers in my face. "I asked you a question."

"What?" I hadn't heard it.

"Who do you work for?"

I checked with Eagle. He gave a quick shake of his head.

I said, "Nobody."

Herne narrowed his eyes. "Don't fudge with me." Except he didn't say "fudge."

My mouth soured. "We'll get out of your hair. I mean fur."

"Excuse me?" His eyes went hard.

"I...I mean hair. We were just leaving."

"Right. You tell that fudging mayor to mind her own business. She's barking up a dangerous tree. The boss don't like people interfering with his income. And if I see either of you again, I'll make sure it's the last time." He reached out and flicked a lock of *my* hair with two fingers.

I flinched away.

Eagle put the car in gear and pulled away from the curb.

I watched Hunter Herne in the side mirror until he was out of sight. He stood there, staring at us with murder in his eyes.

"Why didn't you say anything?" I shouted.

"Calm down," Eagle said. "I didn't need to say anything."

"Oh my god!" I swatted him on the shoulder.

"Put your seatbelt on." Eagle leaned away from me but kept his eyes on the road.

I huffed a frustrated sigh and did as I was told. Once I had strapped myself in, I crossed my arms over my chest.

"It was worth it," Eagle said. "Sometimes, if you stay silent and listen, you find gold. He slipped up."

I thought about that but wasn't sure what Eagle meant. "How?"

"Like how he knows I work for the mayor."

"You work for the mayor?"

"Yeah. And so do you, as long as you're riding with me. He also confirmed that he has a boss, and that his boss is male."

"Oh." I understood what he meant. "Great catch."

"I been doing this a long time."

I felt my shoulders relax. "He's a bully. And what was up with his horns?"

"He's a Herne. Stags shed their rack every year and grow a new one."

"I knew that." No, I didn't.

Eagle glanced at me from the corners of his eyes.

We rode in silence for a few miles. Eagle turned the car toward my Mom's house. He was taking me home.

"Hey! What about waffles?"

"Some other time. I got to go see the mayor."

I frowned. "Fine." Back in high school, my friends and I decided that "fine" was a euphemism for "Fudge you." We'd used it a lot back then, with teenage glee. It was no less satisfying to say it to Eagle.

Another thought occurred to me. "If I work for the mayor

too, I deserve a raise."

"You don't get paid."

"Exactly the problem."

"You want to get paid?" Eagle kept his eyes on the road.

"Yeah."

Eagle pulled his lips in. "Let's see how it goes. We're going to the cave later, after the miners leave for the day."

"We've been up all night!"

"That's the job. Whiners don't get paid."

I scowled at him. "What time?"

"Not sure yet. I'll text you. Be ready." He pulled the car to the curb in front of Mom's house then turned in his seat. "You held your own with Herne. Kept your cool."

"Um, he touched my hair."

"Yeah. I saw. Now get out of my car. I need to go."

I slammed the door extra hard once I was out.

CHAPTER 22

MUSE *learns to let go.*

I t's good to be a cat. I've never enjoyed my otherworldly form. I can't image why humans find bipedal locomotion so interesting. A strong wind or a scolding look can knock you off your feet.

I don't enjoy being naked without my fur. Long-story short, I was pleased to be home.

As always, Greta was sleeping in the fluffy cat-bed. I considered trying to curl up with her, but the last time I'd tried, it had ended in tears. Stubborn as she is, she refused to scoot over, and I ended up rolling awkwardly onto the floor. I don't do awkward. At least not in my cat form. I had lashed out at her, and she awoke in a foul mood. I didn't need that again.

I took some well-earned time to clean by belly, undercarriage, and paws. My journey to find Old Tom had befouled me with alley grime—very much beneath me, both literally and figuratively.

I was finishing off the food in our dishes when I heard a car door slam. I figured 'What the heck,' I'd go see who it was. I wasn't bored, but I didn't have anything else to do either. So, I bounded up onto the window-seat and peered out.

Diana was standing on the sidewalk. She'd emerged from a vehicle driven by an ape. More important was the presence of Mr and Mrs Garrett. They were walking up the street with a cat cage.

My tail went straight down. My ears straight up. If I'd had any, my balls would've pulled up tight. (Yes, they're gone. I mourn them every time I clean myself.)

I ran to Greta, arriving with a full-body slide into her bed—and her. *Wake up, Greta!* I mrowed. *You have to hide. Those people have come back for you.*

Talking with Normal cats doesn't work, and Greta was Normal. She couldn't hear the words in my head. All she caught were mews, meows, and mrrrows. My body language should have been enough to alert her to trouble, and I was thinking *very* loudly—dammit!

Greta, the tease, stretched from the tip of her paws to the tip of her tail. She yawned.

I poked her with my nose. *Up, up, up, up. Follow me.*

She stood and took another leisurely stretch.

I backed away, toward the hiding place I'd identified for just such an occasion. *Come on. This way.*

She sat and started to clean her face.

No! I yowled. *Greta, this is it. They're going to take you away from me! You'll be on your own again. Your only hope is to hide.*

She couldn't be bothered.

The front door opened, and a crowd entered the house. They were laughing and talking about fires, cats, and kidnappings.

That was ancient history to me.

Greta's ears perked up, and she stood.

Finally! She got it.

C'mon, c'mon, c'mon!

I ran around behind Greta and put my cold nose where the sun don't shine.

She scooted away and hissed back at me.

Move it or lose me! I hissed back at her.

Without warning, Greta took off running—in the wrong direction.

I was too stunned to keep up with her, much less overtake her.

She zoomed to the Garretts. I made it to the doorway just in time to see her stretch her paws up Mrs Garrett's leg.

My heart fell as I realized I'd lost her.

Everything moved quickly after that. Mrs Garrett put Greta in the cage, and they left.

I returned to my perch on the window-seat and watched them go.

Greta didn't look back once.

My heart ached.

I told myself that she was better off without me. After all, I was nothing but a trouble magnet.

◆ ◆ ◆

CHAPTER 23

KITTY *nurses Muse.*

I craned my neck to see around the cracks in the windshield. To avoid the police, I took side roads and drove like a granny. The last thing I needed was a ticket, or worse, an impounded car. Diana didn't have enough sway at the sheriff's office to get me out of that.

I dropped the car off at my house and stopped in for a few minutes. When I walked in the door, Muse waiting for me in the foyer. He sat there and yowled as if he'd just lost his best friend. I bent and petted him.

"What's the matter, baby? Has Diana not fed you?"

The poor kitten rubbed his whole body against my leg. I picked him up. "Are you crying because you missed me?" I kissed his head and scritched behind his ears. "What a sweet boy you are. My Muse. Are you feeling better? I bet you were so frightened at the vet, honey, but you're home now. You're safe. I'm here."

I carried him into the kitchen and set him on the counter. "Let's see what you did to yourself, precious." I turned him so I could examine his stomach. "Oh goodness," I said. "Two whole stitches. How did this happen? Sweet boy. Would you like something yummy to eat." I set him down, so he wouldn't try to jump. Then, I prepared a couple dishes of wet food—one for him and one for Greta.

"Greta! Komeneatskeeee! It's breakfast! Yay!" I set the dishes on the floor. "Well, brunch, technically."

Muse made a beeline for the bowl and started eating. "Good kitty," I said, petting his head. "It's a positive sign that you're hungry. You must be okay."

"Greta!" I walked around, calling for her. She didn't come.

Standing in the doorway to the basement, I called down.

"Greta! C'mere, honey! There's food!"

"Mom!" Diana shouted from below. "Greta's gone! I'm sleeping!"

I descended the stairs. "Gone? What do you mean, gone?"

Diana was curled up on the bed. Her hair was wet from the shower, and she was dressed in sweats and a t-shirt. Her dog was cleaning itself beside her. "Her parents came to get her. The Garretts."

"Oh! I'll miss her sweet face, but I'm glad she's with her people." I crossed the room and sat on the edge of the mattress.

Diana peered at me. "Why are you here? Is Aunt Martha back?"

"No. I think she's in England. I had a tiny accident with the car."

"What? Are you okay?"

"Physically, yes. My windshield went head-to-head with a foul ball, and the windshield lost."

"How bad is it?"

"Bad enough that I need a new windshield."

"You can't drive it like that."

"Duh. I'll get an e-taxi back to Martha's. Why are you sleeping this late?" I straightened the bedspread.

"I was out all night with Eagle."

My eyebrows shot up. "Out? As in..."

"As in on a stakeout. I can't tell you more than that."

"Why not?"

"It's confidential."

"I'm your mother."

"Still confidential, Mom."

"Is this safe?" I searched her for bullet or knife wounds. She had nicked herself shaving her ankle, but that was all I saw.

Diana hesitated before answering.

I put a hand on her forearm. "Diana? Daughter? Is it safe?"

"Well...as safe as anything these days. It's important. That's what matters. And Eagle is with me."

"Who are you watching?"

"Just some criminals. No biggy."

"Criminals like Kyle?" Diana's husband was a white-collar criminal and wouldn't hurt a fly—not physically, at least.

"Low blow, Mom." Diana turned away and rolled to sit up on the opposite edge of the bed.

"I meant 'non-violent.'"

"You don't have to worry." Diana stood. "Do you mind? I need to get dressed. Eagle might text me any minute. We're going out again this afternoon."

"On a date?" I asked, hopeful.

"No." Diana had that impatient tone she sometimes gets with me. She enunciated. "Not on a date. On another stakeout."

"Okey-doke. Well, I've had a busy week." I turned my back to give her privacy. "I saw a warlock about my curse."

"A warlock?" She sounded surprised. "You?"

"Yeah, why not me? I do things."

"No, I just mean it's not like you to be so... so..."

"So what?"

"I dunno. So self-caring, I guess. You're always helping others."

"I do self-care. I get my annual mammo. Speaking of which, have you—"

"Yes, Mom. What was the warlock like?"

"Scary. And amazing. She couldn't help me, though. Said the curse was all in my head."

"That's what I said."

"Pfah."

Diana's phone pinged. She had finished dressing and moved to it. "It's Eagle," she said. "Five minute warning." She thumb-typed her reply then headed up the stairs. "I need to get my shoes on."

I followed her, of course.

Diana went to the foyer and sat on the bench where she'd left her sneakers. "We can give you a ride to Martha's if you hurry."

"Really? That would be fantastic, but only if you're going that way. I wouldn't want to—"

"We are. More or less."

I raised both hands, palms toward her. "Ask Eagle if it's

okay. I'm going to grab my stuff and give Muse a treat. It'll just take a minute."

"Oh, that reminds me," Diana said. "The vet prescribed antibiotics for Muse. It's in the fridge. He needs it twice a day. The dosage is on the bottle."

"Did you already give him some?"

Diana chortled. "You kidding? He wouldn't let me near him."

I muttered, "Smart cat," as I walked away.

"What was that?"

"Nothing!"

Ten minutes later, I was ready. Those ten minutes gave Diana the time she needed to walk Mimi, so I didn't feel too guilty delaying them. I had packed a bag of toiletries and the cat carrier—containing Muse. I couldn't leave him behind. He was so pitiful. He needed extra love and cuddles, and Diana was a dog person. She'd have thrown food at him and called it a day.

Muse could stay with me at Martha's. Smaug and Faffy might even appreciate some excitement.

Besides, after the day I'd had, I could use a three-kitties-in-the-bed kind of night.

Turns out this Eagle fella isn't much of a conversationalist. I did my best, but Diana kept shooting me dark looks over her shoulder. I tried to engage him on the topic of their investigation.

He was cagey.

No wonder Diana didn't want to date him.

By the time I got out of the car at Martha's, I'd decided I didn't trust him. Professional courtesy could have prompted him to be more friendly. I was, after all, a fellow detective.

So what if I hadn't solved many cases?

Since he wouldn't talk to me, I didn't bother to tell him my suspicions surrounding Harold's sketchy death. After all, the saying wasn't 'Tit for nothing.' It was 'Tit for tat.' I didn't get any tat, so I gave no tit.

I couldn't blame him if he considered me a rival. After all, I'd beaten him to the reward in the Case of the Missing Brat. That was my previous caper. The money had come in handy. More than handy. It was allowing me to pay my mortgage and bills for several months.

I wished I had another case like that.

Helping Martha had no financial benefit. It was, however, the right thing to do. Who would I be if I didn't help my friend?

Nevertheless, I hoped Martha would return soon so I could take on a case with a reward. In the meantime, I was determined to solve the mystery of Harold. Who tore up Martha's house? What was this about a second wife? And had Harold been murdered, or had it been an accident?

No matter how much Diana poo-pooed me, I knew there was a big mystery to solve.

I unlocked the door, stepped inside, set down Muse's carrier, relocked the door, and went to the alarm box.

It should have been beeping at me. Confused, I squinted at it. Had I forgotten to set the alarm when I left? I must have.

The curse had struck again.

I armed it then searched the place. "Martha? Are you here?"

No answer.

The kitties came out to investigate Muse's carrier, so I figured there was no one else there. Smaug and Faffy would've been hiding if there were. Nevertheless, I turned on every light in every room I entered.

Giving a cat medicine can challenge even the most experienced catsitter. First, I get his food ready so I can give it to him immediately after the medicating. Eating distracts him from his outrage. Plus, it'll ease your mind when he chows down. You didn't hurt him.

Once the cat has figured out your plan, he may fight you tooth and nail. Or at least squirm like the devil's whispering in his ear. I clear a space for the pill-giving—either on a counter or on the floor. Use the same spot every time, so the cat becomes acclimated to what's going to happen there. Have everything you need within reach and readied. Both you and your cat want this to be over fast.

If it's a liquid, it's easy. The vet will provide you with an eyedropper to use. Double-check your measurement. Then just feed it in.

Pills are the worst. Back in the olden days, you took your chances and stuck your fingers in the cat's mouth to get the pill on his tongue. Modern technology has made that technique obsolete.

I have a set of "pill poppers." They look like chunky toy syringes, and there's no needle. Instead, they pop the pill out with a pfoosh of air when you push the plunger. The cat bites the plastic, instead of you.

Personally, I hate taking pills dry, so I always suck water into the plastic syringe before I stick the pill in the tip. That way, the kitty gets a drink to wash down the pill. The trick is to push the plunger with a slow, even pressure. That way, your cat has the chance to swallow, and you don't put water in his lungs. Slow and easy. Pausing a moment to let the cat catch up is a good idea.

Once I have everything ready—and I do mean everything—I pull him in close and use my body as a barrier so he's stymied. I keep one palm against the far side of his face. This prevents him from turning his head away. Keep your hand flat, fingers together, or he may accidentally nip a stray finger.

You don't have to hold the cat tightly. You just have to become an immovable wall between him and freedom. Be especially gentle around his neck, and take care not to catch his tail between you and the edge of the countertop. You want him to trust that you're not trying to kill him.

If the cat is a violent objector, you can wrap him in a towel to restrict his use of claws. Make sure his legs and tail aren't twisted in there. If he's in any discomfort, he's going to fight even harder.

To get your cat to open his mouth, open yours. The cat will understand and open up. This only works once, though. After that, he's learned his lesson, and you have to apply gentle pressure on the side of his mouth with the tip of the popper. Depending on how stubborn he is, you may find this takes patience.

No matter how careful you are, cats are skilled at hiding the pill under their tongues then spitting it out as soon as you turn your back. So, keep an eye out for stray pills, especially if you have more than one cat. All it takes is one curious nose to get a pill stuck to it. From there, a lick and it's inside the wrong cat.

Lots of love, kind words, and petting goes a long way to reassure your cat once you've finished torturing him. I can say with some confidence, however, that no cat understands the words, "It's for your own good."

◆ ◆ ◆

CHAPTER 24

DIANA *gets all shook up.*

Mom could not have been more annoying. The moment she was in the backseat of Eagle's car, she leaned forward and grilled Eagle about how he'd gotten started being a detective, what it was like, where he found his cases, how much he charged, whether he'd ever been shot, what his current investigation involved, why his car wasn't full of pee bottles...

It was incessant. And the worst part was that she ignored my signals.

Eagle, to his credit, didn't dump her on the side of the road. He answered with vague replies, shrugs, grunts, and glances into the rearview mirror at her.

I was so embarrassed.

Once she was out of the car, I faked a small chuckle. "Moms, huh?"

Eagle slid his eyes to me but didn't turn his head. After a tense moment, he said, "She's a kitten compared to mine. One of my superpowers is dodging nosy-mom questions."

I relaxed.

As a token of my appreciation for his understanding, I blurted, "I told her I graduated from college, but I never did."

Eagle's eyebrows rose. "You went to college?" He navigated the car back onto the road.

"I started out in Physical Education. Did that for three years, including a couple student-teacher stints. I wanted to teach kids, ya know, how to take care of themselves. It wasn't like that, though. They wanted me to learn all the sports, and I do mean *all* the sports. I hate sports. I find football, hockey, and rugby inane and stupidly violent."

Eagle listened without comment.

"Basketball's okay. That, at least, doesn't encourage assault. Tennis is cool. Any game that has the word 'Love' in the scoring can't be all bad, right? Track was fine, but they taught that the focus was on beating the other person, not on beating your own highest score."

Eagle grunted.

I said, "And then there were the kids with no self-esteem. They thought they were fat, or ugly, or weak, and it made them do horrible things to their bodies—just so they fit whatever notion society had of attractiveness. It was heartbreaking. And you know what?"

Eagle shook his head.

"Kids can be hateful creatures. They bully and sexually harass one another all the time. They're the worst! And when you call them on it, they act like it's no big deal."

Eagle and I fell into a temporary silence. I was deep in my thoughts, and he was being himself.

I debated whether to tell him. I hadn't even told my mom. But something about Eagle encouraged sharing secrets.

I said, "When I was student-teaching at a high school, a girl in my class killed herself. Her classmates had bullied her and made her hate herself. I quit after that. Walked away from the internship and changed majors."

Eagle spoke for the first time. "You felt helpless."

He was partly right. "Yes, and I also felt endangered. Like, if I became a teacher, I'd be opening myself up to so much suffering. I'd be miserable for the rest of my life. And I'm no hero."

"You were young."

I studied Eagle's profile. His expression held no emotion, no judgment, no sadness. It was matter-of-fact.

"I was. And so, I turned to computers. I was already a major geek anyway, so learning computer science was a no-brainer. It's a lot easier to wrangle a bunch of cables, motherboards, chips, and cards. They may crash, but they don't break your heart when they do." I paused a beat then added, "Well, sometimes they do, like when your hard drive crashes and you lose all the love poetry you wrote to that one boy who didn't even know you existed." I sighed.

Eagle gave me another side-eye, a smile tugging up one side of his mouth.

We arrived at the parking site and got out of the car. Sneaking through the woods with Eagle was a singular experience. I believe I've mentioned that he's kind of ginormous. So, if I stayed on his heels, I avoided the slapping branches. When he halted in place, however, I slammed right into him. Not complaining, mind you.

We snuck up to the main entrance of the cave and waited. The sun was setting, casting the forest in shadows.

It wasn't long before the miners emerged and headed down the trail. They weren't talking, exhausted after a hard day's work.

Once they were out of sight, I started to follow them.

Eagle put his hand out to indicate we should wait.

I kept my voice low. "What?"

"Let's make sure they're all out."

Made sense, so we waited. It was only five minutes, but it dragged like an hour. I was bored and itchy. I made a mental note to bring mosquito repellent the next time.

When I could no longer take the silence, I asked, "What are we doing?"

His response was, "C'mon." He eased out of hiding and headed toward the cave entrance.

I followed. "The miners went that-a way. Aren't we going to follow them?"

"Not this time."

We turned on our flashlights, crept into the damp dark, and walked to the mining site.

"You see anything that stands out?" Eagle asked.

"Am I looking for anything in particular?"

"You know, like sparky stuff. Magick."

"Only that giant ephemeral dragon guarding the gold."

Eagle turned his eyes toward me, his expression stony.

I shrugged and smiled. "Kidding. No, I don't see anything sparky."

Eagle scowled a moment longer at me before he moved forward. His target was the shed. The miners kept the door locked with a thick padlock.

I kept look-out while he picked the lock, and when he stepped inside, I positioned myself in the doorway. "What do you expect to find?"

Eagle shrugged. "Don't touch anything." He pulled his leather gloves tighter onto his hands.

The wooden shed was twelve feet square and made of unfinished boards. It had a door but no windows. One wall held shelves and a bench. Another held hooks with shovels, axes, and sledge hammers. The miners had DIY'd a desk out of a sheet of plywood placed across two saw horses. Old coffee mugs, pots, pans, pens, a packet of toilet paper rolls, and hand tools cluttered the desk. Mining equipment took up the rest of the space.

I said, "Looks like they don't store any paperwork here."

Eagle stepped over equipment on his way to the back.

"Anything?" I asked.

"Nah." He turned in place and retraced his steps. When he arrived at the door, he said, "Step inside for a minute."

I did.

Eagle shut the door and shone his flashlight on the back of

it. I did the same with mine. The miners had hung a calender there. They had made notations on it, numbers and words, especially on weekdays.

"Here," Eagle held out his flashlight to me. "Hold this."

I took it from him. It was slippery in my gloved hand, so I tucked it in my armpit while I removed my glove.

"Point it at the door, please." He gestured as if I were an idiot.

I stowed the glove in my pocket. "One sec!" I re-situated the flashlight in my bare hand. "Like this?" Sarcasm dripped from my tone.

"Yeah." If he'd noticed my snark, he didn't acknowledge it. He took several photos of the calendar's pages.

I had to close my eyes against the flash. It lit up Eagle's face, the calendar, and the back of the door with blinding harshness. An outline of the tableau ghosted the back of my eyelids for long seconds.

Eagle pried the flashlight from my hand. "Got it. Let's get out of here. I want a better look at these pictures."

The shed door squeaked when I opened it, and I led the way out. I had a half second to glance around before my head spun and a wave of dizziness overcame me. In the next instant, a loud rumble surrounded us. It grew in volume, and the ground beneath my feet shook.

Eagle grabbed me by the collar and jerked me backward into the shed's doorway.

Rocks of all sizes fell around us, splashing into the river and bouncing off boulders.

I latched onto Eagle to keep from falling over. "What's happening?"

"Earthquake." One hand on the doorframe, one on me, Eagle swayed from side to side, trying to maintain his balance.

A large stalactite broke loose from the ceiling overhead. Eagle jumped back into the shed, dragging me with him. The hunk of stone barely missed the shed.

Inside, tools were rocking and falling inside. They added to the clatter.

Eagle grunted as my knees gave out. I ended up squatting with my arms over my head. To his credit, he didn't release my collar for an instant.

After an eternity, the rumbling stopped and the dust settled. Eagle and I waited in silence, barely breathing.

I was the first one to speak. "Can we go now?"

"Yeah."

I took a few steps out the door. My foot slipped on loose gravel, and I almost fell.

Eagle still had hold of my collar. He steadied me. "Watch your step."

"I thought I was." I shuffled my feet over the rock and watched the ground ahead of me. We picked our way out of the cave. It wasn't until we were in the forest that I realized we hadn't locked the shed back up. I could've mentioned it to Eagle, but I was afraid he'd go back in there. I just hoped the miners would think they'd forgotten to lock it. The earthquake would explain anything else we'd disturbed.

"I have to pee," I announced. In the aftermath of the excitement, my bladder needed to reduce its load.

Eagle waited while I went behind a bush. It was primitive, and I wished for one of those toilet paper rolls I'd spotted in the shed.

When I returned to Eagle, he had his foot up on a log and was wrapping a length of bloody cloth around his calf.

I ran to him. "Oh my god. Are you hurt?"

"It's nothing." The liar—he'd lost the color in his face.

I wondered whether I could carry him out. "You faint on me, and I'll leave you here."

"I'm fi..." He wavered on his feet.

I tucked my shoulders under his arm. "Give me the keys. I'm driving."

"Okay. But if you damage my car, I'll bury you out here."

"Got it."

◆ ◆ ◆

Mrroooow!
— anonymous

◆

CHAPTER 25

MUSE *has a bad day.*

That day didn't have a single ray of sunshine in it. Kitty introduced me to her clients, calling them Faffy and Smaug. I knew immediately we wouldn't get along. Not like Greta and I had.

Don't get me wrong. I had no desire to smack the resident layabouts. It wasn't their fault they were clichés. I was bored, and the last thing I needed was a couple of fluff-heads following me around like I was royalty.

Of course, I *am* royalty, but that's beside the point. I wanted to disappear into my misery. My Greta was gone. Forever. My broken heart required that I have time to wallow and whine. I needed to eat myself into oblivion.

Kitty insisted I swallow pink liquid that tasted like dog butt. She said it was for my own good. As if. At first, I resisted, but when I let her know my displeasure by yowling, she took advantage and stuck the dropper into my mouth. I was doomed. Hoisted on my own petard! Curses!

Afterward, I sniffed my way to the food dishes only to discover more disappointment. The grub was mediocre at best. Same ol' kibble. Same ol' chicken in gravy. I started working up a hairball to express my utter despair. Nothing came up but chicken and gravy.

Kitty was in the bathroom, so—out of ennui—I went and peeked in.

A vast expanse of furless skin made my eyes bulge.

"Hi, Muse," Kitty said. She hiked one leg into the tub then

the other. Never underestimate the potential horror of a cat's-eye-view. I averted my gaze—too late.

"Did you come to keep me company?" The water splashed as she settled in.

I took off like a bullet toward the living room. Let's just say, I had a zoomie. I came to an abrupt halt and checked every corner for...anything interesting. Disappointed, I sat and licked—

That was when my whole body crackled electric. My skin twitched. My fur itched. I listened. Nothing. I looked. Nothing. I hunkered down, belly to the floor, and hissed.

Kitty was in the bathtub—beyond my reach.

Faffy and Smaug had disappeared.

I was in trouble—knew it as well as I knew my own butt.

I had just enough time to yowl a warning before it hit.

My entire world shifted. The ground moved under me. I stuck my claws in the cracks between the floorboards then changed my mind and ran for cover.

First, I tried the darkness under the couch, but it started shaking, so I bolted. A great rattle, clatter, and thumping made a chaotic cacophony, and the Earth itself groaned as if in pain.

The sky was falling! Something rained down on my head, and I did an about-face, streaking toward an armchair.

I was all reaction and instinct. My brain had gone into self-defense mode.

The assault continued for an eternity, and when it stopped, I waited for it to start again.

Once the world had truly settled, I realized what had happened.

We'd had an earthquake.

By then, I was tucked under a heavy bureau, panting and tense.

I was alive. Was Kitty?

Squeezing out from under the furniture proved harder than getting in. It was proof that where physics end, adrenaline takes over.

An obstacle course of broken glass made my progress slow, but I made it to the bathroom door. My brain created several scenarios in which I found Kitty crushed or drowned or dead from shock.

Before entering, I called, "Marco!" Of course, it came out as "Meow-o!"

I expected her to call "Polo," which she sometimes does. Instead, Kitty asked, "Muse? What's happening? Are you okay, honey?" After much splashing of water, she appeared in the doorway, eyes wild with worry. She was wrapping herself in her robe, a blessing for which I was grateful.

I sat and let her bend to pet me. She seemed unharmed. I didn't smell blood—only lavender bath salts.

"Oh my goodness," she said, taking in the chaos the earthquake had caused. Picture frames had fallen off the walls and accounted for the shattered glass. "Faffy! Smaug!"

I stayed beside Kitty after that—not because I was afraid for myself but because I might have to shield her, in the event of another earthquake. I was ready—mostly.

We went into the bedroom.

Kitty called, "Faffy! Smaug! Where are you, honies?" She got down on hands and knees and peered under the bed. "There you are, babies. It's okay. The earthquake is over. You can come out now."

They didn't budge. In the darkness beneath, they were black shadows with shining eyes, huddled together against the apocolypse.

"It's okay, kitties. You're safe." Kitty stood up and rested her hands on her hips, turning in place to survey the damage. It wasn't too messy in the bedroom. She picked up her phone and bapped at it. After a listen, she said, "Hi, honey. It's Mom. Just checking in. Everything okay? Did you feel the earthquake? Call me when you get a chance." She put the phone down.

I jumped up on the bed. Sitting in cat-lotus, perfectly balanced on my butt, front paws together in a feline mudra, I closed my eyes and buried my emotions in the litter box of my mind. I'd deal with losing Greta and having the sky fall on my head at a later time.

Kitty froze. I heard her go silent and opened my eyes. She'd spotted the thing that had emerged from the lake. When I saw it, my blood ran cold.

◆ ◆ ◆

CHAPTER 26

KITTY *meets a little lady.*

She looked like something that had crawled out of a television. With her head bowed, her wet hair hung to her waist. When she peeked out from behind it, however, her eyes were soft, scared, and olive green. She couldn't have been older than nine or ten, and she had skinny legs that were too long for her body. They stuck out from under a faded blue t-shirt two sizes too big. It had the flaking transfer of a sea turtle on it.

"Hi," I said. "I'm Kitty. Are you okay? Did the earthquake frighten you?"

The girl nodded.

"What's your name, sweetie?" I bent to be more on her level.

"Merlynn."

Muse jumped off the bed and circled wide around behind her, back arched, tail electrified.

"How'd you get in here, Merlynn?"

She pointed at the master bedroom. "Where's Father?"

"You're looking for your dad?" Why do we always repeat children's questions back to them? It's inane.

Merlynn nodded.

Muse snuck close and sniffed the girl. He pushed up on his tippy-toes, hissed, and then bolted away.

To cover for his rudeness, I asked, "Who's your father?"

The child narrowed her eyes at me. "He lives here. Harold."

"Harold Fishgiven?"

Again, she just nodded.

"Oh." I didn't know what else to say. To my knowledge, Harold Fishgiven had never had children. But then, I'd had met a woman who claimed to be his *other* wife. Harold must have been sixty-three or -four when Merlynn was conceived. It was possible. Men's bodies didn't close-up-shop the way women's did.

I stared at the girl, unsure of what to say. She was dripping on the floor.

"Wait here." I returned to the bathroom and pulled a big soft towel off the rack.

When I offered it to her, she accepted it but didn't seem to know what to do with it.

"May I?" I gently used one end of the towel to dry her skinny arms. Her skin was pale, as if it never saw much sun. Around her neck, she wore a small chunk of raw gold on a leather cord.

She didn't resist. "I need to talk to my father. Can you make him come here?"

"I'm sorry, honey." I crouched in front of her, drying her legs.

The girl hovered on the verge of taking flight.

I was a stranger. It wasn't my place to reveal that her father had died. "Your dad is...not here. But you can tell me instead. Maybe I can help?" I hugged the damp towel to me.

Merlynn inhaled through her nose, summing me up. "He has to stop." She sidled around me, moving toward the door.

"Stop what, Merlynn?"

"Tell him he's going to ruin everything."

I didn't understand what she was talking about. Before I could get more out of her, I needed her to calm down. "You know what," I said. "I have cookies. Would you like a cookie?"

She had to think about it, but in the end, she agreed.

I led the way to the kitchen. "So, do you have any brothers or sisters?"

"Four sisters and one brother."

"Is Harold their father too?"

"Yes. My brother lives in town now, but the rest of us are together."

"I see. And are you the youngest?"

She nodded. "And I'm the smartest."

"I believe it. Where do you live?" I took my time getting out a plate and a glass.

"Talyllyn." Merlynn hopped up onto a stool at the island bar as if she'd done it many times before.

"Oh." I gave her my best winning smile. "Where's your house?"

She avoided answering my question by saying, "I'm not supposed to be here."

"Do you come here to visit your father a lot?" I removed the milk jug from the refrigerator and poured her a glass.

Merlynn shrugged. "Sometimes. Mama doesn't want me to, but…"

"But he's your father."

"Yes. He's kind to me. His Martha is too."

"Does Martha know you're his daughter?"

"No. Father said to never tell her. He said it would kill her."

I brought the cookie jar closer and spotted Muse hovering nearby. "You don't like cookies," I told him. "But I'll get you a treat. You've earned it, brave boy."

He made no sound. He sat still as a statue, his stare locked on Merlynn.

I placed two oatmeal cookies on the plate, then carried it and the glass of milk to the island, and set them in front of the girl. "Here you go, sweetie." I backed away a few steps and leaned against the counter. "You have a beautiful name."

"Mama gave it to me."

She tasted the first cookie. If her enthusiasm was any indication, she liked it.

I pulled a broom from the kitchen closet and began sweeping. I wanted to make sure there were no stray glass shards to cut kitty or child paws. I also hoped it made me less intimidating. The worst thing you can do with a skittish cat is meet their eyes. I assumed the same was true for kith children.

"Merlynn, did you ever give your father any presents? Something to eat, maybe?"

With crumbs on her chin, she spoke with her mouth full. "No. Where is he? Why can't you make him come here?"

Abruptly, she turned aside and stopped blinking.

I followed her gaze to the sliding glass door. The lake woman stood there, soaking wet, dressed only in a short cotton shift that clung to her body. She may as well have been naked again. I recognized her. Rhiannon.

The woman was worried. Then, she got angry. She put her palm on the glass. The contact caused a purple spark, and she pulled back as if it had hurt.

The girl scrambled off the stool and hurried to the door. She tugged on it, but it was locked. "I'm in trouble. Please, tell my father what I said. Don't let him wake up the giant."

I joined her and locked eyes with Merlynn's mother, Harold's other wife. Her anger showed on her face. I smiled to put her mind at ease and unlocked the door.

"Let's invite her to join us."

"No. She can't come in. Father's ward lets me in."

"What ward?"

Merlynn latched onto the belt of my robe. "Warn Father. It's important." She pulled the door open and walked out into the circle of her mother's arm.

Rhiannon asked me, "What did you tell her?"

"Nothing." I placed myself in the doorway, hands over my heart. "The earthquake upset her, so I tried to calm her down. We talked about her siblings, and I gave her cookies and milk."

The lady of the lake ran her gaze up the wall and around the door. "Thank you, but she does not belong in this realm. Please, do not encourage her. The balance will be restored soon, but until then, she must stay close to home."

"What do you mean?" I asked, hoping to keep her talking.

Rhiannon paused to glance over her shoulder at me. She was unsure about speaking to me. "You are kind. You should leave here. There are destructive forces that want to drown us in their evil. Go home, and keep your family safe. There is nothing more you can do. Leave it with us."

With that, she guided her daughter to turn around and descend the stairs.

I said, "I still don't understand. What are you talking about?"

Rhiannon didn't acknowledge my question, but Merlynn looked back one more time. She flashed her eyes at me.

I went out onto the terrace and watched them go. They walked into the water and disappeared under the surface.

My detective senses were wriggling in the back of my neck. Something was not right.

Muse meowed behind me. He was sitting in the doorway, head tipped to one side.

"Oh, buddy. I promised you treats, didn't I?" I went back inside to fulfill my promise, to coax Faffy and Smaug out from under the bed, and to clean up the mess—again.

Muse followed me everywhere. The earthquake had shaken him.

Who am I kidding? It shook me. My nerves were jangled. There's nothing like the feeling of the earth moving beneath you. We take it for granted that we're on solid ground, but we are as vulnerable as ants in an anthill.

I was pondering the fragile nature of our world when I heard Diana shouting on the front porch. "Mom! Mom!"

I nearly jumped out of my skin.

A second later, the doorbell started ringing with a vengeance.

◆ ◆ ◆

CHAPTER 27

DIANA *rescues Eagle.*

I hauled Eagle from the car to the front porch by myself. He could only put weight on one leg. He'd tied a cloth around the other—a cloth that appeared less than sanitary.

An eternity passed before Mom opened the door. Eagle was getting heavier by the moment, and his face had lost its color.

"Mom! Help me!"

"Oh my goodness! What happened?" She got under Eagle's other arm.

"He cut his leg."

"I'm fine," Eagle insisted.

Mom took one look at the bloody rag and asked, "Why didn't you take him to the hospital?"

Eagle latched onto me with his big paw. "No hospital."

I gave Mom a wry smile. "That's why."

Together, Mom and I got him into the bathroom. We sat him on the toilet lid. I stood back and watched as Mom applied first aid. She unwrapped the rag, examined the wound, rinsed it, disinfected it, and then bandaged it.

Eagle's girlish blush returned.

Mom then turned *me* in place, examining me.

"I'm okay." I was covered with dust, but otherwise, I wasn't injured.

Mom hugged me. "Was this the earthquake?"

"Yeah."

"Where were you?"

"On a stake-out."

Mom harrumphed and refocused on Eagle. "Well, young man, your wound doesn't seem *too* bad. You should get stitches, but if you don't mind a n*asty* scar, it'll probably close up on its own." She gave Eagle her mom-look. "I'm guessing you weren't in the car when this happened?"

I chewed on my lip. Of course, I'd have told Mom everything if Eagle weren't there. I decided to fill her in later.

When Eagle shrugged in reply, she got the message. She gestured to indicate I should wait there while she shuffled off to do something mysterious.

I met Eagle's gaze, and he gave me a direct order with his eyes. He didn't want me to tell Mom about our adventure. To avoid him, I grabbed a washcloth and cleaned my face in the bathroom sink.

Mom came back with Uncle Harold's walker. "Sorry, I didn't find any crutches. You can get those at the drugstore."

Eagle, of course, tried to refuse and stand on his own.

That was when he met the full force of Mama Kitty's will. "Stop. You're going to open it up again. Give it some time to knit, okay? Let's sit in the living room. I'll make us something to eat."

Eagle—observant man that he is—picked up on her tone and did as he was told. He used Harold's walker to get to the couch and only grumbled once when I helped him get his leg up onto a pillow on the coffee table.

I switched on the TV and found the evening news. The earthquake and its aftermath occupied center stage. Six people had ended up in the hospital and one had died. Experts were explaining how earthquakes happen, what to do when one does, and the history of the Cascadia fault line. They were making predictions for when the Big One would hit. We learned that the epicenter had been in the Coast Range Mountains, a few miles inland, east of Wyrdwood.

We watched in silence. Mom fussed over dinner. Eagle scowled.

"5.2 on the Richter Scale, huh?" Mom asked, coming into the living room with a platter of tater tots she had cooked in the air fryer. "We're pretty close to the epicenter."

"Yeah." Eagle pushed himself up straighter on the couch.

I carried place settings and water glasses to the coffee table.

Mom, being her usual nosy self, asked again, "Where were

you when it happened?"

I looked at Eagle, and he at me. He shook his head the tiniest bit.

I said, "In the national forest." It wasn't *exactly* a lie. "We took shelter in a shed. Eagle cut his leg on a digging tool."

Mom grunted. "Your tetanus shot up to date?"

Eagle grunted back.

"What were you two doing out there?"

I brought ketchup, mustard, and hot sauce to the living room. "It's a case we're working on, Mom. We can't talk about it."

"Why not? It's just me." Mom stopped what she was doing to lean against the counter and stare at us.

I crossed my arms in defiance. "We've had this conversation. It's someone's private business, that's why. We'd be breaking a confidence."

She sighed and returned to her task. "Well," she said, "I have something I'd like to discuss with you."

"Oh, here we go," I said under my breath, expecting her usual nagging.

"Your Uncle Harold was murdered."

I shook my head. "Mom."

Eagle had shifted his full attention to Mom.

"I'm telling you, someone murdered him. I'm pretty sure."

I was confused. "By food poisoning? But the M.E. determined it was an accidental death."

"Sure. That's what the killer wanted."

I helped her carry the turkey subs to the living room. "Why do you say it was murder?"

"Well, the killer tore apart the house, searching for something. It's better that it was. You should've seen it when I first got here. They didn't find what they were looking for, either. Martha said it was wrecked already when the caretaker discovered the body."

"Might've been thieves?" I suggested.

"No. Nothing stolen."

"Maybe it was his *other* wife, wanting mementos?"

Mom shook her head and finished chewing before replying. "She can't get in the house. Harold put a ward on it to keep her out."

"He didn't trust her?"

"Apparently not. Though it's probably less about her being dangerous and more about him not wanting her to run into Martha. Rhiannon—the second wife—is a Lady of the Lake, and she had no hesitation telling me she was his wife. Harold fathered her six children."

Muse took off at full speed and zoomed from the sliding glass door to the couch. He flew along the back of it.

Surprised, we all watched him go.

He launched himself onto the cat tree, startling Martha's cats. After shooting a glare right, then left, he dropped to the floor and scratched madly on an armchair.

"Muse!" Mom scolded. "Stop that!"

Mom's new cat sat and licked a paw.

We waited a beat to see what he'd do next. He gave himself a bath.

To get us back on track, I said, "Six children?"

Mom nodded. "I met the youngest one. Right before you arrived. A girl named Merlynn. She doesn't know Harold's dead. She wanted me to warn him. She knows he was in danger. I didn't have the chance to ask her more. Her mother showed up and took her home."

I chewed on this as I ate. Eagle had said nothing, but he was listening. His brow furrowed.

I said aloud what I guessed Eagle was thinking, "So, what you have is a child who's worried about her dad. A tossed house. And...what?"

"A feeling."

"A feeling?"

"In my gut." Mom wiped the corner of her mouth with a napkin. "Martha thought so too. When she first called me, she said Harold had been murdered."

"Did she say why?"

"No. And she has since changed her mind. She says she was

just upset. But don't underestimate the power of intuition. I know it's not much. But things are too weird around here."

"Weird and murder are two different things. This *is* Wyrdwood, Mom."

"I know."

We ate in silence for a while.

Mom was the first to speak. "Eagle, what do you think?"

Eagle had vacuumed his sandwich and fries. He sat with his water glass clasped in both hands, staring into it as if he could scry the truth. "You got more questions than answers. But you might be onto somethin'. Who had access to him?"

Mom counted on her fingertips. "The caretaker. His daughter, I suppose, though I asked her whether she gave him anything, and she said she didn't. Might've been a business associate. Harold was laid up with a broken hip, and his office is downstairs. They'd ransacked it too. Also, he cosigned a loan for a fella name Ewan Trelor. According to a certain bow-tied wiener, Mr. Trelor has defaulted on it. He can't make the payments."

I asked, "Bow-tied wiener?"

Mom waved me off. "The one who cursed me. Never mind."

Eagle used his hands to lift his leg off the coffee table and set his foot on the floor. "The wife too. She had access, right?"

"She was at her sister's that weekend."

Eagle nodded. "You confirmed that?"

"No, but I've known Martha forever. She wouldn't do this. She's devastated."

Skepticism raised Eagle's eyebrows. "What'd Fishgiven do for a living?"

Mom said, "Harold worked for the TV news. That's why he was gone so often. They'd send him on assignment. He was a producer or something."

Eagle scratched his cheek, mouth open. "Convenient."

"What does that mean?"

"Just sayin'. If I had a second wife, I'd need an excuse to be away."

I blurted, "You have a first wife?"

"No." Eagle curled his upper lip. "I'm not the marrying type."

Mom said, "We never talked much about his job, but he had side projects going too. His own business. A landscaping team he ran. Martha mentioned him meeting with clients in his office."

Eagle sat forward. "You think he was shady?"

Mom shrugged. "He liked his get-rich-quick schemes. It was always something with him. He called himself a part-time entrepreneur."

I was watching a tennis match. Mom. Eagle. Mom. Eagle. Mom.

Eagle suggested, "Maybe one of his business associates killed him?"

Mom considered that. "Come to think of it, Merlynn—the baby girl—asked to me to warn him 'not to wake up the giant.'" She made air quotes.

I smiled. "She's been reading fairy tales."

And just like that, the tennis ball flew out of bounds. I'd broken the rhythm.

With a scolding frown, Mom said, "C'mon, Di. Don't be so Normal. It's far more likely that she overheard something the adults were saying. This wasn't a flight of fancy. What if they killed Harold because he made the wrong person angry? The Giant, whoever that is."

"A pyramid scheme?" A lump developed in my throat. Trauma rising. "They were at my wedding. They met Kyle. Could he have been working with Kyle?"

Mom reached out to touch my knee. "No, honey. Harold would never defraud people. Besides, Martha would have mentioned it if Harold was tied up in Kyle's scheme."

"We need to find out, Mom." A squirrelly unease stirred in my belly.

Eagle stood. He wobbled at first then steadied himself. "I gotta go. Diana, you want a ride home?"

"Sure." I started picking up the dirty dishes.

"Oh, don't worry about cleaning up," Mom said. "I'll take care of it."

"Mrs. Kats," Eagle said, his voice flat. "If I were you, I'd be all over that office. You might find out what got your friend killed."

"I was hoping you guys would tell me I was being ridiculous."

"Follow your instincts, ma'am." Limping, Eagle headed for the door.

"Oh, I will."

I kissed Mom on the cheek as I went by. "I'll call you tomorrow."

She followed us.

I put on my jacket and checked my pockets for my house keys. I pulled out my caving gloves to get to them. I only had one. I turned in a circle, searching for the other on the floor. It wasn't there.

Eagle and I headed for his car.

I confessed, "I misplaced one of my gloves."

"Where?"

"I don't know."

He bobbed his head, pensive.

I suggested, "Maybe it's in the car?"

"Get in," he said. "I'll drive. You search." He opened the passenger door for me.

Before I could sit, a dirty old pickup truck pulled off the shoulder and came down the road. It slid to a halt at the end of the driveway.

Time slowed.

A pistol emerged from the driver's window.

I froze.

◆ ◆ ◆

CHAPTER 28

MUSE *witnesses a shooting.*

The humanoids were eating and talking murder The resident peasants were sleeping on their carpeted tree. I was eavesdropping and guarding the sliding door to make sure the Ladies of the Lake didn't kill us. Someone had to be the adult.

It's clear to me that Harold Fishgiven was a baby donor for a Lady of the Lake—probably the hag who came to the door. He must've entered into a contract with her in his youth. I've seen it many times. Once a month, the mama emerges from the lake and copulates with her donor. Then she leaves. Sometimes, love develops between them. Sometimes, it's a long-term exchange of—ahem—currency.

For the lady, the benefit is obvious. What the man receives in return is less apparent. If I were to guess, I'd say it's equivalent to good luck. The men in question remain successful, healthy, and happy—so long as they keep up their end of the bargain. Not a bad trade-off. *And* you get a clandestine cuddle every month.

Fishgiven wasn't dumb. The fact that he warded his home against the lady tells me he understood the danger, especially if he was hiding the arrangement from his other wife. Creatures like them don't understand landlubber social taboos.

The more I heard, the more I agreed with Kitty. Someone murdered Fishgiven, and my favorite suspect was the Lady of the Lake. Although, the ward was a problem.

After much thinking, I had no choice but to burn off energy. I switched to chase mode and hit the trail running. Up and over, down, through, faster than fast—I was flying! Until I wasn't. Then, I scratched a tree to warn my enemies to watch out.

I followed when everyone walked to the front door, and I sat beside Kitty's ankles. Diana and her gorilla limped to the car.

That was when the maniac pulled up and pointed a gun at us. Yes, I know what a gun is. It's the preferred weapon of maniacs.

I thought, "Huh." It was odd. I felt detached from reality, as if I wasn't in my body anymore. My second actual thought was to save Kitty. I slashed at her ankle with my sharpest claw.

She cried out and stepped aside.

The gun fired.

I hunkered down.

Kitty squeaked.

It fired off again.

My back arched of its own accord. I hate loud noises.

Everyone was scrambling. Diana's bodyguard threw her to the ground and lay on top of her. Kitty pressed against the wall.

I was the only one who noticed that the gunman was aiming high over the house. Furthermore, when he had finished shooting, as he drove away, he tossed something out of the truck.

Diana and the man got to their feet. "Mom!" Diana ran toward the house.

Kitty, with her hand pressed to her chest, slid into the doorway. "I'm okay. Is he gone?"

Diana didn't answer. She grabbed her mom and suffocated her with an intense hug. If that had been me, I'd have been squirming to free myself. Kitty, however, let it happen.

"I'm okay," Kitty repeated. "Are you okay?"

Diana's gorilla limped to the road and stood there with his hands on his sides. He scowled in the direction the truck had gone.

"What just happened?" Kitty asked, not unreasonably. "Why was that man shooting at us?" Kitty had wild eyes. It was not a good sign.

"C'mon, Mom. Let's go sit down. We can explain."

The man named Eagle started back toward the house. He'd left the shooter's discarded whatsit lying on the side of the road. I knew it was important, so I took it upon myself to sprint out to get it. I zipped past him and ran to...the glove. It was a glove for humanoids. I picked it up with my mouth. My plan was to run back with it, but it kept getting tangled in my feet. By the time I got to the porch, Eagle had gone inside and closed the door. He was oblivious, the stupid gorilla.

I was shut out, with a dirty glove in my jaws. I set it on the porch and mrrowed at the top of my lungs.

No one came. I was forgotten. Abandoned. Forsaken.

I tunneled through the bushes and took up a position beneath the bay window. I thought of Greta then yowled again, injecting it with heartfelt misery.

Kitty stuck her head out. "Muse? C'mere, honey! Were you locked out? I'm so sorry!"

I returned to the porch. I had mud on my cheeks and nose, leaves in my fur, and my feet were in an awful state of filth. I'd picked up a few fleas in the bushes, too.

"Oh my goodness. How'd you get so dirty so fast? You must've been terrified, you poor baby." Kitty bent to pet my head.

I sat beside the glove.

Diana joined us. "Is that my glove? I guess I dropped it out here."

From somewhere inside, Diana's bodyguard said, "The shooter dropped it. He was sending us a message."

So, he *had* seen it and hadn't bothered to pick it up. Maybe he guessed it would make Kitty go zoomy.

When Kitty gets the zoomies, she waves her hands around, paces in all directions, and uses too many words. "Tell me what's going on! Someone shot at us. They could've killed us! Who was that? No more secrets! Is this your fault, Eagle?"

Diana, who had experience with Mom Mania, guided Kitty back to the livingroom and sat her down. "I'll make you some tea, Mom. We'll tell you everything."

And so they did. It was a rousing story about caverns, miners, and underground rivers. It made my tail twitchy.

Needless to say, Kitty was not amused. And yet, she was intrigued. I could tell by the spark in her eye.

◆ ◆ ◆

CHAPTER 29

KITTY *and Eli dig for clues.*

Diana was reluctant to leave me alone. Bless her heart. I assured her I was fine.

"I'll lock up tight. Go walk your dog. I don't want her pooping in the foyer." A sense of normalcy had descended upon us. In a way, it was shocking to behave so normally after being shot at.

Eagle was leaning against the doorway to the livingroom, favoring his injured leg. "I'll take you home, Diana, then I'll report this. No reason to get involved with that tonight. I don't think he was shooting *at* us. If he had been, he'd have at least dinged the car."

Diana took a deliberate breath, the kind she takes when she and I are arguing. "You sure?"

"Pretty sure. He didn't hit anything at all."

"Okay," Diana said. "Mom, set the alarm once we're out, will you?"

"I will."

"And keep your phone close."

"Right-o." And I did. I stood at the window and watched them drive away. My heart was still racing. I tried to shut the drapes, only to discover that my hands were shaking. The sight of the tremors broke something in me, and I huffed a sob. My normalcy was a facade, a stoic front meant to hide how shaken I was. In the aftermath, it hit me hard, and I had to sit on the sofa.

Someone had shot at us! He could've killed me! *He* could've killed Diana!

Another burst of adrenaline coursed through me, this time fueled by anger. *How dare he? How dare he shoot bullets at my daughter?*

Clarity spread through my mind.

Muse, who was meatloafed on the back of the couch, relaxing, had already finished his bath. He'd missed a burr on his scruff, so I picked it off him.

"The man in the truck," I said. "I've seen him before. He was the one who broke in here last night." I was convinced. I could see his silhouette in my mind. He had the same thick messy hair and cowlicks.

Muse gave me a slow blink then yawned big enough to swallow his own head.

I spent time loving on Faffy and Smaug with treats and lots of cooing. They didn't seem traumatized by the gunfire, but I made sure they knew they were safe. I put butter on a paw to encourage them to lick themselves. Grooming is to kitties what pacifiers are to babies. It doesn't hurt that they love butter. Muse licked his off my finger, and that soothed us both.

Everyone piled on the bed, and that's where we awoke together the next morning.

After breakfast and the scooping of the pooping, I headed for Harold's office. I needed to find out how Harold was connected to the illegal gold miners. He had something they wanted.

With renewed vigor, I tackled the mess there, making piles of papers and examining each one as I placed it.

On the other side of the house, the doorbell rang. I froze, planning to ignore it.

Whoever it was rang the doorbell again then banged on the front door.

I didn't move. I had no desire to talk to anyone. I was busy.

I heard, "Kitty? It's Eli. Are you there?" He had come around the side of the house. "Hey, Kitty! It's me, Eli! You okay?"

I sat still, waiting for him to go away.

Several minutes passed.

His face appeared at window.

I gasped in surprise.

"There you are!" he said. "Didn't you hear me calling?" He hurried to door and came in. "Hi!" He had a bundle of mixed flowers in his hands.

I sorta smiled.

"I wanted to make it up to you for that dunk in the lake."

"That wasn't your fault." I took the bouquet from him. "They're beautiful. Thank you."

He asked, "You okay?"

"I'm okay."

He scanned the mess in the office. "Did the earthquake do this?"

I decided to tell the truth. It would have been easier to lie, and I admit that I considered it. However, I needed help, and he fit the bill.

I lay the flowers on the desk. "No. There was a break-in."

That took him aback. "Oh." He put his hands on his hips and contemplated the mess. "Did you report it to the police?"

"It happened before I got here. I believe Martha reported it."

"How can I help?"

I smiled for real. "There's a loan contract here somewhere. Harold cosigned for a guy named Ewan Trelor. Martha's estate lawyer needs it."

Eli pushed papers aside with his toe, making an island for himself amidst them. He sat cross-legged. "Is that what the intruder was looking for?"

"I doubt it. Whatever it was, they didn't find it." The moment the words were out of my mouth, I knew I'd made a mistake.

"How do you know?"

"Um," I said, hesitant to say anything to trigger his protective streak. It was too late, though. The cat was out of the bag. "Because they came back again."

"While you were here?" His eyebrows rose to his hairline.

"Kinda?"

"Did you report it?"

"Of course! I called the police right away."

"Mm." Eli looked askance at me.

"I did!"

"No one said anything to *me*."

"Why would they?" I challenged him with my eyes. "There

was no fire."

He stared back then sighed and fiddled with the piles surrounding him. "I hear you. Mind my own beeswax."

"Loan agreement." I waved my hand to indicate the sea of paper. "Search."

"Yes, ma'am." When Eli called me "ma'am," it didn't sound like an insult.

We chatted while we worked. Eli talked about his daughters, his rabbits, and his job. I made encouraging noises to let him know I was listening. I'd forgotten how talkative Eli could be.

"In a few years, I'll take early retirement and make room for the next generation of firefighters. My second-in-command, Jerry, is ready to step up. Only thing in the way is me."

"What will you do with yourself when you retire ?"

"Relax a bit. Spend more time on my hobbies."

"You have hobbies?"

"Sure. My boat. Golf. My rabbits. And the grandkids."

"You have grandchildren?"

"Not yet, but my eldest got married last year."

"You'd make a great grandfather."

"I'd do my best." Eli got up to stretch his legs. He perused the mess.

I stood too. My back ached from sitting on the floor. "I thought maybe Di would give me grandkids, but that didn't work out. I guess I should be grateful Kyle never got her pregnant."

"Kyle was an idiot."

"Still is. Di is divorcing him."

"Smart girl. Cut all ties."

"Yeah, she is." I walked over to one of the overturned filing cabinets. "I'm proud of how she's handling it." I bent and tried to stand the metal cabinet upright. It was heavier than I'd expected and had wheels, so it tended to slide rather than tip.

Eli appeared at my side. Once we had it back on all four wheels, we pushed it against the wall, perhaps a bit too firmly. A click sounded, and the wall shifted.

I was staring at a secret panel.

Eli pushed the cabinet to one side so we could access it better.

The panel popped open a smidge when you pressed on it, like some cabinet doors do. It swung on hinges and revealed a hidden room. I crossed the threshold and found the light switch. The room had no windows. Though narrow, it extended the length of the house. A workbench held a variety of tools, and a giant safe stood at the far end.

In one corner, a circular staircase rose to a hatch in the ceiling. I tried to imagine where that might come out and realized it was under Harold's bedroom closet.

"Harold had a Bat Cave," I said.

Eli gave an exaggerated nod. "Or an evil lair. I'm jealous."

The intruder hadn't found the hidden room. Everything there was in order. Even the earthquake hadn't disturbed it. It contained the evidence we needed to prove that Harold had been involved with the miners. Even a cursory glance around revealed it. On the wall over the bench, Harold had pinned a map of the basalt caverns and their entrances.

He had various small tools, a precise jeweler's scale, a box of plastic baggies, and sheets of adhesive labels. A notebook detailed their scores by date, weight, and purity.

"Holy cow," I said. Puzzle pieces were falling into place in my mind. Harold had been involved with the miners and had maybe even made his fortune with them. It made sense that whatever the intruder had been searching for was in the hidden room.

Had he killed Harold? Had Harold died to protect his stash?

Eli stuck his index finger in his mouth and sucked on it.

I raised my eyebrows. "What happened? You okay?"

He blinked then smiled. "Yeah. Fine. This chisel is sharper than I expected." He pointed out a tool lying on the bench. It had the slightest dusting of shiny gold upon it.

"Is that gold?" I leaned closer.

"It is indeed."

It surprised me that it was glowing in the dim light. Not

magickal. Just golden. A fine layer of dust with a smear in it where Eli had touched it.

"Let me see your finger," I said.

"No, really, it's fine. It's no worse than a paper cut."

"Well, you should wash your hands and put antiseptic on it. Who knows where that thing has been?"

"Yes, ma'am," Eli said warmly. He walked over to the safe. It was an antique, stood about four feet tall, and was solid metal. The door had a rotary combination lock. "I don't suppose you have the code, do you?"

I shook my head. "No. Martha might. I'll ask her when I talk to her." I joined him and bent to examine the lock. He did the same—at exactly the same time.

We bumped heads.

"Oh!" I pulled back.

Eli laughed.

I laughed too, and it felt amazing. I couldn't remember the last time I'd spontaneously laughed. "I'm so sorry," I said.

"No, I'm sorry. Are you okay? This ol' noggin' is pretty hard."

"Mine's pretty hard too. Or so I'm told."

Eli put his hands on my shoulders and pressed his lips to my forehead. He held them there a second longer than necessary, and in my surprise, I let him. He smelled smoky, cedar and pine, as if he'd just left a campfire. It was woodsy and pleasant.

I shifted my weight. "Thanks," I said. "All better." I turned my attention back to the bench. "Maybe Harold wrote the combination on a sticky or something?"

"You may be right."

I opened the ledger and flipped through its pages, back to front. Nothing. "Maybe he used his birthday? Or Martha's?"

"Can't hurt to try. Do you know what they are?"

I did, though I had to guess the year. I spun the dial around to the right a couple times to reset it, then stopped on "10"—Martha's birth month. I turned the knob the way we did the lock on our lockers in high school. Muscle memory kicked in. When I arrived at the last number, however, it didn't open.

I tried the same with Harold's birthday. Then, their wedding day. Nothing.

Eli did his best as well. The safe remained closed.

We searched the hidden room but found no code. We did find more evidence of Harold's involvement with the miners. He'd contracted them and was paying them with a percentage of the haul. One name stood out from the list of employees: Hunter Herne. Every mother in Wyrdwood knew about the Hernes and hid their daughters whenever one was around. They weren't abusive. Their charm and persistence broke down the resistance of even the shyest virgin.

Hunter Herne III had been in my class at school, and my mother would've installed a chastity belt on me to keep me out of his clutches. I'd thought it was love. He'd said it was love. We were both wrong. Fortunately, I met Eli before the Herne bagged me.

I knew Herne the Third had died in a car accident years earlier. So, I figured this one was Herne the Fourth. In the same grade at school as Diana. I'd warned her about the Hernes, and she'd stayed far away from him. My good girl.

"I think the mayor might be interested in this," I said.

"Why?" Eli was pulling up a corner of the map to peek behind it.

"They're mining illegally. I think."

"Do you know where they're doing it?" He pressed the corner back down.

"Some cave somewhere. Probably the one on that map." I indicated it with a sassy smile.

Eli laughed. "Probably. You going to tell Mayor Violet?"

"I should. This situation is getting sticky. One of the miners might have killed Harold."

"What?"

I filled him in on my suspicions then added, "I don't have enough evidence to convince the sheriff's department it was murder, though."

"Why would one of his employees kill him?"

I shrugged. "I can imagine several motives. What if he was cheating them out of their fair share? Or they figured out they could keep all the money if they got rid of him? Suppose he was getting ready to shut it all down and retire. Or maybe his luck ran out, and the mine dried up?"

Eli grinned. "You've thought this through."

"All I know is that the Herne was in Martha's house the other night, looking for something. Maybe he tossed it the first time, too."

"I'm hearing a lot of guesses. Why don't we take a break? We can talk it out over lunch. My treat. I'll come back with you, and we can finish searching for those loan papers."

My stomach loved that idea, and I never say no to a free lunch.

◆ ◆ ◆

CHAPTER 30

DIANA *meets Eli.*

The fire chief and my mom were looking cozy when I arrived at Martha and Harold's that evening. They answered the door together.

"Hi, Di," Mom said. "How was work?" I'd texted her to let her know I was coming to spend the night. I didn't want her to be alone. Heck, who was I kidding? I didn't want to be alone. Safety in numbers, am I right?

"It was work." I'd kicked off my morning by cleaning up the paperclips that Brenda had spilled. She was out of the office, or I might've been tempted to escalate our feud.

I was holding Mimi in my arms. She wriggled at the sight of a tall stranger—the fire chief—and growled low in her throat.

"Mimi!" I scolded.

"She smells the cats," Mom said. "Di, you remember Elias Kariuki, right?"

"Yes, hi. Nice to see you."

"Hi, Di." Fire Chief Elias Kariuki was an attractive older man. His skin was seasoned by his genetics plus years fighting fires and basking in the sun. Muscled, perfect posture, and completely bald, he struck an impressive figure. He asked me, "How are you?"

"Keeping busy."

The fire chief smiled slyly. "So I hear." He looked at Mom, and I saw the affection he had for her. It knocked me back on my heels. "Well, I better get going." He walked out onto the front porch then wagged his index finger as if he remembered something he'd forgotten. He pulled a folded sheet of paper from his back pocket.

"I found this." He handed it to Mom.

She scanned it then stared up at him in surprise. "The loan agreement!"

"Confession. I came across it this morning."

Mom's mouth fell open. "Eli! Why didn't you say something?"

"I wanted more time with you." A contented expression played across his face. He was pleased with himself.

My eyebrows rose.

"Naughty," Mom said. Flirty. She was flirting with him!

"I'll call you." The fire chief turned to leave. As he passed close to me, Mini-Mimi broke into a round of yappy barks, her stumpy legs paddling to get free.

"Settle down, Beavis." I pulled the dog against my chest.

"Thanks for all your help," Mom called.

The fire chief didn't look back but raised his hand to wave. "My pleasure entirely."

As I would expect, he was driving a ginormous 4x4 truck with a crew cab—in bright red.

Mom stayed in the doorway, watching him pull out of the driveway. She waved.

I said, "You like him."

With a side-eyed glance, Mom asked, "Is that an accusation?"

"Just an observation."

Mom turned and walked into the house. "He's an old friend. We dated in high school."

"You and the fire chief? You, madam, are an enigma." I squeezed past her, eager to get inside. "What did he find?"

Mom shut the front door and followed me, reading the paper in her hands. "It's the loan agreement between Harold and Ewan Trelor. Martha's estate lawyer needs it. Ah, poo."

"What's the matter?" I set Mimi down and headed for the kitchen to get her some water. She would only drink out of her favorite bowl.

"I'm no expert, but this looks legit. If Ewan defaults on the loan, Harold is on the hook for the balance. That's the opposite of motive."

"What do you mean?" I laid my tote bag on the counter and dug in it for Mimi's dish.

"Ewan doesn't benefit from Harold's death."

"You still think Harold was murdered?"

"I do. Even moreso now. I have to show you something."

I filled the dog bowl then followed Mom into Harold's bedroom. She opened the closet and bent to study the floor.

I leaned around the doorframe. "What are you doing?"

"There's a trapdoor here." She moved aside some shoes and an old braided rug.

"Wow. Where does it go?"

Mom pulled on the recessed handle, and the trapdoor opened. It had hydraulic hinges. Someone had built it with safety in mind.

Down in the hole, I saw a spiral staircase. "Has this always been here?"

"No." Mom headed down the stairs. "Harold had it installed so Martha could have a guest room. It's his office. Come on down."

Once she was at the bottom, I stepped onto the staircase as well. It was sturdy, functional rather than decorative. Typical Harold.

I descended into a narrow work room.

"This," Mom said, "is a hidden room. Harold's secret. Eli and I found it."

"Awesome." I had no idea why she seemed so excited.

"We found evidence that Harold was the one in charge of the mining operation that you're investigating."

That surprised me. "Seriously?"

"Dead serious. I've got personnel records and this ledger that tracks the gold they found every day."

"Okay." I caught up with her thinking, noticing the tools, examining the ledger, and beginning to feel like the joke was on us.

"Di," Mom said, grabbing hold of my forearm. "The man who shot at us. Hunter Herne. He was the one who broke in. He was the one I saw. I'm sure of it."

It was a lot to take in. My instinct was to poo-poo what she was saying because, well, she cries wolf. But I couldn't deny that it was making sense.

"What if," Mom said. "What if he killed Harold?"

"Why would he do that?"

"Look." Mom walked over to a giant safe. It had to be older than me. Maybe even older than her. She began turning the dial on it. "It took some fiddling, but Eli and I figured out the combination." The dial's rattle had heft, importance, like a warning, a foretelling of doom. On the last number, it clicked, and Mom pushed down the handle. Using her entire body, she leaned back and tugged on the door.

I found myself staring at a wall of money, bundled and wrapped in plastic. A shelf at the top held baggies. At first, I thought they were drugs, but when I picked one up and examined it, I discovered it was gold. Dust, flakes, and nuggets.

"We weighed them," Mom said. "Those are one ounce each."

"How much is it worth?"

"Lots."

I put the baggie back as if it were fragile. "So...Uncle Harold..."

"Yes. He's the one running the mining operation."

We stood in silence for a full minute, staring into the safe.

Never had I seen so much money. It made my heart race.

When my thoughts had become more ordered, I asked, "Does Martha know about this?"

Mom shrugged. "I don't think so." From the safe, she removed a manila folder. Inside was a handwritten letter.

It said:

Under the light of the full moon, promises made, vows spoken. On each new moon, Harold Fishgiven and Rhiannon of Talyllyn will rendezvous in their sacred cove for the sole purpose of creating children. For as long as the covenant is unbroken, Harold will profit from the blessings of the Ladies of the Lake. He will thrive, prosper, and be protected. Twice, he will be forgiven. If he fails to appear three times, the pact will end. Thus, Rhiannon of Talyllyn becomes the wife of Harold Fishgiven. From this day forward, may they be fruitful and multiply.

Both Harold and Rhiannon had signed it.

"This is so weird," I said. "How old was Harold?"

"He must have been in high school."

"When did he meet Martha?"

"Well, they were friends all throughout school. But, as Martha tells the story, they didn't fall in love until the end of their senior year."

"Was he already married to Rhiannon when he got with Martha?"

"I'd guess so, yes."

"Dang."

"Exactly."

I pulled my phone out and took a few pictures. "I have to call Eagle. He'll want to see this."

"Can you put him on speaker?"

"Sure."

The phone rang a couple of times before Eagle answered. "Diana."

"Eagle. You're on speaker with Mom. You won't believe

what she found."

Mom smiled, proud of herself.

I said, "I'm sending you photos. Harold Fishgiven is the big boss in charge of the mining operation. There's a crap-ton of money here. And gold. He hid it all in a secret room."

Mom nudged me in the shoulder. "Tell him about the ledger."

"He kept records. What should we do?"

Eagle paused a beat before replying. "I'll ask the mayor. We're going out to arrest the miners."

"What? I want to go too!" I held the phone closer to my mouth. "I've earned it."

Again, Eagle paused, but he conceded. "I suppose. All right. I'll swing by and grab you on the way. I'm meeting the mayor and sheriff's deputies at the station."

"I'm at the Fishgivens' lakehouse with Mom."

"Got it. Be ready. I'm on my way." He hung up.

Excited, Mom squeed. "Eee!" She wrapped both hands around my bicep and shook it. "The bad guys are going down!"

I looked at her calmly, hiding my amusement. "Settle down, Beavis." Of course, I was squeeing inside too.

◆ ◆ ◆

CHAPTER 31

MUSE *holds his tongue.*

I perched regally out of the way as Diana prepped for the takedown. She borrowed one of Martha's blouses and painted her face. You'd have thought she was going to a fancy ball. Kitty followed her, chattering about the solving of the mystery. She was convinced that the stag man had murdered Harold.

"It must have been him," she kept saying. "Who else could it have been?"

Who else, indeed? They say that money is the root of all evil. They also say that Hell hath no fury like a woman scorned. And I was still in the Murderous-Lady-of-the-Lake camp. It's common knowledge throughout the multiverse that poison is a woman's weapon.

Diana's gorilla didn't come to the door. She was watching for him and ran out as soon as he pulled into the driveway. Eager. Either she had her prey—the miners—in her sights, or she had her prey—Eagle—in her sights. I wished her luck on catching her mouse.

I catnapped for the five minutes of peace we had before a knock on the patio door roused me. Through half-lidded eyes, I saw the bottom-feeder child from the lake. She stood there dripping, hands around her eyes and pressed to the glass, looking for—I presumed—Kitty.

When Kitty went to see who it was, the creature took a step back and started talking.

As Kitty opened the door, the girl's voice became audible. "... kill them all. Stop them. Please. Mama said they might not come back. She said goodbye. Please. Do something."

Kitty stared at the child in surprise then crouched to be on her level. "Calm down, Merlynn. We'll figure this out. Your mama is in danger?"

"Yes." Merlynn nodded so hard I was afraid she'd damage her brain—if she hadn't already. "It's the miners. They're evil. They're waking up the giant. Mama's going to stop them—whatever it takes. WHATEVER IT TAKES!"

The child's eyes grew huge and moist. Her tongue tangled in her mouth, and she let out a strangled sob.

I wriggled my body into ready pose, just in case I had to pounce. She was about to explode.

"Okay, okay," Kitty said, using her soothing voice. "Don't worry. I know what to do." Kitty went to the charger and picked up her phone. "I'll call the mayor. They're going to arrest the miners today, so they can protect your mama, too." She held the phone to her ear, waiting, then said, "This is Kitty Kats. Please call me back A.S.A.P. It's urgent, related to the miners." And she quoted a series of numbers. It didn't sound like she was speaking to a real person.

"The miners hate us," the lake child said between hiccups. "They killed..." She trailed off into more sobs.

Kitty crouched beside the stinky, water-logged beast and asked, "They killed someone, honey? Who did they kill?"

Another sob prevented Merlynn from answering.

Kitty petted her.

Whispering, the child finally said, "My Auntie Sallipose. In the caves. She tried to warn them about the giant, and they... She's gone."

I moved closer to Kitty, in case she wanted to pet me, too. She didn't. Instead, she pulled out her phone and pressed more buttons. She held it in mid-air, and it said, "You've reached the office of Mayor Violet Bagley. There's no one here to take your call. Please leave a message or call back between the hours of ten and six, Monday through Friday. If this is an emergency, call Lost Lambs at..."

That was when I stopped listening.

Smaug and Faffy had emerged from their hidey-holes to sniff the puddle spreading around the lake child's feet.

I watched with mixed fascination and horror as Faffy took a

tentative taste of the water. It smelled of water weeds, fish poop, and death to me. Conflicted, I was in awe of Faffy's courage and also disgusted with myself for not having thought of it first.

Kitty drew my attention back to her. "Honey, when you say 'giant,' what do you mean?"

"The ever-living source under the mountain. The Fates put him there to sleep. He can't wake up. He'll be so mad."

The gravity of our situation struck me. I knew about the giant. It was a massive being, but not a Jack-and-the-Beanstalk giant. No *Fee Fi Fo Fum* silliness. More like Cathulhu and *Die Die Die Die*. When the Fates moved Wyrdwood from the old world to the Oregon Territories, it came along for the ride. Its inherent magick fuels the wards that keep Wyrdwood safe, but it's as dangerous as a nuclear reactor. One meltdown, and 'Hello, Apocalypse.'

Kitty asked, "And the miners are waking it up?"

The swamp monster nodded.

"And the earthquake?" Kitty was getting it.

"The giant."

"And your mama is going to stop the miners?"

"Uh huh." The creature from the lake produced so many tears, I was beginning to think that if someone squeezed her, she'd squirt in all directions.

Kitty stood and paced, thinking so hard her neck was turning red.

I followed her, back and forth, careful not to get under her feet or be anywhere she might fall if she passed out.

On the third round trip, she made a decision. She used her phone again. "Yes, I need an e-taxi, please." She told them her destination was the grocery store. I hoped she was going to buy canned salmon.

As soon as she put the black box back in her pocket, it rang. Kitty took it back out and tapped it.

A man's voice resounded in the room, startling everyone but Kitty.

"Mrs Kats, this is Jake Lamb from Lost Lambs. You called the mayor?"

"Mr. Lamb, I need your help."

"What's happening, Mrs. Kats?"

I meatloafed and let my mind wander to happier times as Kitty relayed what we already knew.

◆ ◆ ◆

**I learned everything I know
from my cat.**
— T-shirt

◆

CHAPTER 32

KITTY *heads into danger.*

I took Merlynn back to the lake's edge and ordered her to return home. I only hoped she'd do as she was told. She had dropped quite a responsibility in my lap—saving her mother from the miners. I already knew first-hand what murderous criminals they were, and I suspected they had not only killed Merlynn's auntie but also my friend Harold. Foolish man's luck had run out, and his nefarious friends had come for the gold. That was my working theory, anyway.

Jake Lamb had instructed me to stay home and wait for him to call me once it was over. I thought about Rhiannon, though. What did she hope to accomplish? She couldn't reason with those criminals. Was she walking into a trap? Would there be a shoot-out? And what about Diana? She'd been heading that way, too. If Rhiannon put the miners on alert, would Diana get caught in the crossfire?

A car honked outside.

I'd forgotten that I'd summoned an e-taxi. I didn't even

bother to set the alarm. I pulled the door shut and ran to the driveway. I was acting on pure motherly instinct.

As soon as I was in the backseat, the driver said, "Grocers, right?"

"No." I leaned forward. "Do you know where the basalt caverns are?"

The driver eyed me in the rearview. "Sure. Everyone who went to Wyrdwood High knows where they are. You wanna go there?"

I nodded. "Yes. Take me there."

"Those caves are dangerous."

"I'm aware." I sat back. "Just take me, please."

"All right." He pulled out of the driveway. "Your kid there?"

I met his eyes in the rearview mirror. "Yeah, you might say that."

My heart hammered in my chest. My skin buzzed. I watched the scenery go by and counted the minutes to when we'd arrive. The car smelled like french fries. It made my stomach gurgle.

Something soft brushed against my ankle.

I recoiled from it—as much as I could in the small car.

A pair of black ears with tufts at the tips peeked over the seat's edge. It was Muse.

"What are you doing here?" I asked, breathless.

Muse just blinked slowly at me.

The e-taxi parked in a dirt clearing alongside a red pickup and other cars.

"You sure you want this, lady?"

"Yeah." I didn't see a cave. "Is this the place?"

"You betcha. The mouth is up that path there, in the woods. I can take you home. Or to the grocer. Just say the word."

I rested my fingers on the door handle. "No, I need to do this. Can you drive my cat, though?"

"Your cat?" The driver twisted to look over his shoulder.

Muse had jumped up beside me.

"Just take him back to the house where you picked me up, please? I'll pay for a second ride."

"Why'd you bring him?"

"I didn't. He...snuck in."

"You want me to leave him on the porch or what?"

"Yeah, that'll be fine. He's used to being outdoors." I slid out in such a way that Muse couldn't follow. "Stay here, baby. This nice man is going to take you back to Mildred's. You can't come with me." I petted his head as I squeezed my bottom half out of the car, backing out. "I'll give you a bunch of treaty-treats when I get home, okay?"

The moment I was out and about to shut the door, Muse sprang.

I pressed my palm against his head and stopped him. "Muse! No!" I held him at bay with one hand, sliding my arm out as I closed the door.

I thanked the driver with a wave.

Muse appeared in the window as the e-taxi pulled away. His ears and tail were down, and he was scowling at me.

The basalt cave entrance was a sharp-edged maw with a dark, unfathomable throat. As I approached the lip, I got the feeling I was about to be swallowed whole.

I'd gone twenty feet in when the light from outside dwindled to almost nothing. I kicked myself for forgetting to bring a flashlight and used my phone instead.

The cavern was quiet but for the sound of dripping water. It smelled of minerals, stone, and wet. Before long, I came to the underground river. It had carved a gully in the basalt.

Aloud, I murmured, "I don't like this. Where is everyone? Where are the sheriff's deputies? Where are the Ladies of the Lake?"

"Sheriff's deputies?" A male voice echoed in the cavern, louder than necessary and closer than comfortable.

A shadow emerged from behind a craggy rock.

"Did I say sheriff's deputies?" I took a step back. "I meant..." I didn't find an appropriate comeback, and it wouldn't have mattered if I had.

The man brandished a gun, shutting down my ability to

think. "Move." He indicated I should go further in.

"Why?" I squeaked.

"Don't make me ask twice." The man loomed over me. Strong, not fat, he wore several layers of thick working clothes and wading boots. He was a miner.

"Technically," I said, "you didn't *ask* the first time, so—"

"Go!"

I went.

We followed the river, sticking to the bank. I lost my footing a couple of times on the slippery, rough, rock floor. My captor did nothing, of course, to help stabilize me. He just watched as I teetered and stumbled my way forward. On the plus side, he had a better light source than I did, though he tended to swing it away and leave me blind. I kept my phone's flashlight on, just in case.

A glow lit the cave walls ahead. The closer we got, the brighter it got, until we didn't need flashlights any more.

A handful of people gathered around a campfire near a shed. Seeing a shed in the cavern was surreal, but I realized it held their mining equipment. They had invested in the illegal operation.

"Hey, boss!" shouted the miner behind me, making me jump to high heaven.

He had the other miners' attention, including the Herne's. Hunter Herne the Fourth looked so much like his father. For a moment, I was transported back to school and a ghost of those youthful feelings resurged. It passed. Herne's antlers were less like devil's horns and more like faun antlers. They had a long way to go, but the magickal outline of what they would become was visible and impressive.

The miners cussed like sailors. I won't repeat that part. The Herne used ungentlemanly words in reference to me. The important part was that he wanted me brought to him.

"Hello!" I ventured, hoping to bluff my way out of the pickle I was in. I waved.

All I got in return were glares.

My captor and I made our way to the group.

"Who the hell is that?" a female miner asked.

The Herne crossed his arms. "I know her. She's involved with the mayor's private dick." He stared into my eyes. "Guess you didn't get the message."

"Boss," said the miner with the gun. "She said something about the sheriff."

That changed everything. Electric menace exploded outward from the Herne and ricocheted around.

I hadn't thought it possible, but the Herne's attention bore directly into my eye sockets. "Talk. What do you know?"

I licked my lips, searching for the words that would get me out alive. "Oh my goodness," I said, breathless.

As if on cue, there was a commotion from the cave mouth, and the echo of boots approached. Someone shouted, "Freeze! Wyrdwood Sheriff's Department! Put your hands on your heads!"

The deputies were behind me. When I turned to look, the Herne lurched forward and spun me roughly until I had my back to him. He held me against his chest. The acrid aroma of hard work and barbarity wafted off him.

I felt cold metal press against my temple and tried to turn my head to see what it was.

The Herne shook me and held me even tighter, up on my tiptoes.

"Come any closer, and I'll blow this B...I...T...C...H's head off."

Except *he* didn't spell it. Sorry.

◆ ◆ ◆

CHAPTER 33

DIANA *gets a shock.*

I was bored. Chief Deputy Nick—my boss—had ordered Eagle and me to stay in the car, in the parking lot. It was entertaining, watching the deputies roll out of their vehicles, check their weapons, then proceed in drunken formation along the path toward the cave. They weren't drunk, but their formation was. I made a mental note to suggest to Nick that they perform drills to tighten up their ranks.

Then it was quiet.

Then it wasn't. We heard distant shouting.

A deputy ran out of the woods and went to his vehicle.

Eagle and I got out of the car simultaneously. *Our* formation was slick.

"What's going on?" Eagle called to the deputy.

"No reception in there," he said. "I need to call for reinforcements." He fumbled with his keychain, attempting to open the car door.

"Okay," I said. "Frowny emoji."

"You two should leave. This could get dicey." The deputy slid in behind the steering wheel and reached for the car's radio. "This is WSD5 requesting back-up at the basalt caves. We have a hostage situation. Send a negotiator...and a sniper."

I turned unblinking eyes on Eagle. He was watching the deputy, a scowl on his face.

❖ ❖ ❖

CHAPTER 34

MUSE *takes a leap.*

The instant the strange man opened the door, I bolted. I ran as fast as my powerful cat legs would take me. I leapt onto the front porch, zoomed over the railing and through the bushes, and then sprinted back toward the car. I slid to a halt on the side of the road just in time to see it pull out. I would not follow it there. Too dangerous. Cars had grown as stealthy as dragons in recent years. Quiet. Too quiet.

I foomphed over onto my side in the dirt and lay there panting. I was furious—at myself.

How could I have let Kitty stop me? She was out there without backup! I'd lost my edge! If she died, I'd... I'd... I'd...

I felt my heart racing in the tips of my ears.

Kitty was all alone.

Dejection, then desperation, and then determination shook me—each in turn—and an idea tumbled out of my genius.

I remembered the torc Old Tom had given me.

With my eyes half-lidded in sly focus, I willed myself into the Interstice.

It worked.

And I promptly horked up a hairball. I wasn't used to the disorientation of interstitial travel.

For the next leg of my journey, I had to focus even harder. I'd only seen the clearing once—from the back of a moving car.

I shoved down all doubt, rebuilt the scenery in my mind, then dove through the veil toward it.

What was the worst that could happen?

◆ ◆ ◆

CHAPTER 35

KITTY *bides her time.*

The Herne was so much taller than me that his arm hitched up under my chin. If he squeezed any harder, he'd be strangling me. His aura was hot, his body hard, and his hand firm on my shoulder.

I lifted up on tiptoe to ease the pressure.

Mind, this all happened in a matter of seconds.

Everyone was shouting.

Someone shot at the deputies. A miner.

The deputies returned fire.

Herne shot at the deputies.

A deputy went down.

A miner went down.

And there I was, caught in the middle, a captive observer. My entire front body was exposed.

The gunshots echoed in the cavern, and I put my hands over my ears. I wanted to close my eyes but found they wouldn't obey my command.

The river rushed and overflowed its banks.

Someone shouted, "Hold your fire!" The gunshots dwindled to one, then none. Even the miners paused.

An ethereal glow lit the river water, turning it a periwinkle blue.

I didn't understand what was happening, but I knew it was magick.

From the water, several beings emerged. Covered in cream-colored cowls, they walked out of the river and onto the shore or onto rock outcroppings. Their light came from under their covers. At first, they resembled ghosties, Halloween costumes, but the sheets were robes with hoods. Their naked bodies were visible through the fabric, and one had long red hair.

That one turned to face me—and the Herne.

It was Rhiannon.

Everyone stared, watching the Ladies of the Lake for longer than the gunfight had lasted. In shock.

The Ladies were not of this world, not from Reality. That much was obvious. And they were not pleased.

One deputy—the one Diana had said was her boss—took a single step forward. The act set him apart from his teammates who were standing there with their mouths hanging open. He took the lead.

Rhiannon raised a hand as if conducting a symphony.

"Ma'am," said the deputy in charge. "I need to ask you to—" He and the other deputies dropped to the ground like bags of kitty litter.

The Herne's arm tightened on my neck. He dragged me to one side, taking cover, and tucked his gun between us, at my lower back.

I latched onto his wrist in an effort to loosen his hold. I may as well have been tugging on an iron bar.

Someone shot at the Ladies. A miner.

The Ladies shot back. With magick.

One by one, the miners who dared to shoot fainted—unconscious.

The only sounds in the cavern were the rushing of the bloated river, the beating of my heart, and the Herne's breath. It huffed harsh and quick near my head. His chest rose and fell against my back. The pulse in his wrist was racing as energetically as mine.

The Ladies of the Lake had an agenda. They positioned themselves in a circle and made magickal marks at their feet. Their body's luminescence grew until the cloaks they wore became lanterns. They weren't in any hurry.

I assessed the situation. The deputies and miners were breathing—unconscious, not dead. Thank goodness. I worried about the ones who'd been shot. Were they still bleeding? Would they die?

"We have to get help," I whispered to the Herne, my chin

bumping against the Herne's hard arm as I spoke.

He growled. "How do you s'pose we do that? Phones don't work in here."

I hoped that Rhiannon's spell hadn't affected the deputies further out in the cave.

A miner, who had hidden herself behind a rock, tried to escape. She scrambled over an outcropping and splashed through the water at the river's edge.

Rhiannon turned.

Before the miner could get out of sight, Rhiannon cast her spell, and the miner collapsed on the bank.

"So much for making a run for it," I commented wryly.

The Herne grunted. I felt it in his stomach muscles against my back.

Rhiannon cast a wary eye around the cavern then returned to doing whatever the Ladies were doing—their preparations.

"What do you suppose they're doing?" Energetic tension was building around us.

"No idea. But it ain't good."

"You know," I said, "they're here because of you."

"What?" The Herne kept his voice low too.

"Uh huh. You've been disturbing the giant under the mountain."

"By panning for gold? Don't be dumb."

"I don't understand how it works, but that's why they're here. To stop you."

When the Herne didn't reply, I asked, "You're the one who broke into the Fishgiven house and searched it, right?"

"Yeah, so?"

"Did you find the gold?"

"How do you know about the gold?" The Herne squeezed my neck.

"Everyone knows...about the gold. It's a no-brainer. You worked for Harold, didn't you?"

"Yeah, the old bastard."

"If Martha had been home, would you have hurt her?"

The Herne shifted his weight and loosened his hold on my

throat. He sighed. "Don't worry about her. She's tougher than she pretends. When Harold kicked the bucket, I saw an opportunity to take over the operation. To do that, I needed his fence's contact information. And his stash of the gold." The Herne rested his cheek against my head. "His widow caught me, and I underestimated her. She got the drop on me with her gun. I figured she'd call the sheriff, but she made it clear as ice that she's the boss now."

I required a moment to assimilate that. "You're lying."

"Nope. What I'm doing is surviving this bull... and then moving to Vermont."

"Did you kill Harold?"

"What do *you* think?"

As it turned out, I had no time to think anything. The Ladies faced into the mountain, lifted their voices, and raised their hands upward, singing an ancient song. I didn't recognize the language. It sounded like gibberish to me, and yet it filled the cavern with harmonic resonance. Magick radiated off them.

The beauty of it brought tears to my eyes.

The Herne sucked in a breath.

It was a lullaby. I understood what they were trying to do. Their magick expanded, their voices swelling until the sound came from all around. I settled on my skin and in my head, my chest, my heart. I was becoming the song.

Out of the corner of my eye, I caught movement.

Another miner, who had also been hidden, stalked forward. His face twisted with terror and madness. In his hand, he held a stick of dynamite—the old-fashioned kind—and the wick was lit.

I cried, "No!" and raised my hands as if that could stop the blast from hitting me.

The Herne pulled me back, shielding himself behind my body.

◆ ◆ ◆

CHAPTER 36

DIANA *has only one option.*

I ran to the deputy in the car. He was saying, "I repeat, we need reinforcements. Hostage is a woman in her fifties, name of Kitty Kats."

The dispatcher said, "Say again, WSD5. That was Kitty Kats?"

"Yes. That's really her name. Kitty Kats. She's a civilian."

I stopped on a dime. "What? No. What?" My head was spinning. "Mom?"

The radio crackled. "Is that Kats with a C? Z on the end?"

"I don't know," the deputy replied.

I grabbed him and sunk my nails into his arm. "What's going on why is my mom here who has her where is she?" The questions rolled out of me without punctuation.

The deputy blinked up at me. His fingers dug at mine, trying to get me to release him.

"I need you to calm down, miss," he said.

Eagle took me by the upper arms and pulled me off the officer. "Diana." The way he said my name was enough to make me let go. He'd managed to combine a command and a reassurance into that one word.

I turned to face Eagle. "We have to go." I tried to push him aside. It was like shoving a hundred-year-old maple tree. "Eagle!" I tried to skirt around him. He held me in place.

"We'll go," he said. "But not until you settle down."

That was the incentive I needed. Fingers on his chest, I focused on controlling myself. "I'm fine," I lied.

"Just give it a minute to stick," Eagle said. "We're not going in there with you half-cocked."

"We need your gun."

Eagle's mouth almost disappeared when he drew his lips

tightly together. He gave a curt nod.

Through gritted teeth, I urged him, "Let's go."

The deputy had returned to talking with Dispatch.

Eagle went to the car to get his flashlight. I did my antsy dance while waiting for him.

"How the hell did she get involved in this?" I asked, expecting no answer. "What was she thinking?"

Eagle had no answers. He shut his car door and hooked his holster on his belt.

I took the flashlight he offered me, then sped toward the path. He had to run to catch up. When we entered the cave, he said, "Stay behind me."

◆ ◆ ◆

CHAPTER 37

MUSE *needs a do-over.*

I popped out of the Interstice. Wooziness clouded my mind, but I didn't puke.

A woman screamed.

Someone shoved me off an edge into mid-air. I twisted to get my feet under me and landed on soft carpet. I crouched, making myself as small as possible.

"Oh my god!" the woman said. "There's a cat in here. Is this your cat?"

I was in a car. The floor shuddered beneath me, and the smell of old french fries hit me in the nose. I recognized that stank. I had willed myself back into the e-taxi.

I yowled in frustration.

The woman screamed again. She smacked me with something heavy.

On instinct, I hissed.

"Is he black and white?" the driver asked, unable to see me where I was.

"Yes! Is he going to bite me?"

"Don't worry," said the driver. "I know him."

I closed my eyes and tried to concentrate. It took a few seconds, but I managed to 'chute back to the Interstice. I sat there, in my humanoid form and caught my breath. Obviously, I needed practice. It could've been worse.

I'd done it on purpose, I told myself. It was a trial run, I told myself. I had to test whether I could port into a moving vehicle, I told myself. I was smarter for having done it, I told myself. I made the right decision—I told myself.

I had calmed. I was alone and safe. I sat cross-legged and visualized the clearing where Kitty had left me. I visualized Kitty. Her gentle hands. Her pale, splotchy skin. Her warm chubby body. Her cooing voice.

Before I knew it, I was 'chuting again—right out of the Interstice and into...

I landed on cold, wet rock. Smells assaulted and disoriented me. Minerals, water, fresh blood, rat poop...

And Kitty.

I hunkered down and scanned my environs. I was underground. The cavern and the rocks were giant-sized.

Ladies of the Lake. They had their magick going, glowing like lanterns under their sheets. They were humming. It wasn't unpleasant, but they were the Ladies of the Lake, hoarders of fish, drowners of cats.

My hackles twitched. I was out in the open, vulnerable. I scanned the outer edges of the cavern. Kitty was there somewhere. Keeping my belly low to the ground, I followed her scent. It was an obstacle course. Bodies dotted my path, providing cover. They were asleep, which I found odd. They were warm, which I found enticing. But, what a terrible time and place to nap. Still, who was I to judge? I enjoyed naps as much as anyone.

As expected, my stealth, cleverness, and nose served me well. I made it to the wall without incident, glanced around for danger, then—seeing no eyes on me—I leapt onto a high ledge. From there, I had an unobstructed view of the area.

I heard Kitty's voice among a sudden burst of others. They all shouted, "No!"

I spotted her.

She was staring at a man who was throwing a sparking explosive.

My tail poofed to its full glory, and I mrrowed like an air-raid siren.

The exclamation point on my warning was the resounding boom of the dynamite exploding.

◆ ◆ ◆

It's not nice to fool Mother Nature.
Chiffon margarine commercial, 1977

◆

CHAPTER 38

KITTY *'chutes and scores.*

The sky was falling! After the explosion, a great rumbling gained in volume. Rocks rained down on us. The Herne used me as a shield, and I did my best to protect my head. A cloud of dust filled the cavern, and I closed my eyes. I thought of Diana and wondered where she was. I thought of my husband. I thought I was going to die.

The Herne and I cowered against the cave wall. His arms were iron bands around me, but I could feel him trembling. Or maybe I was the one trembling. It didn't matter which.

Then, the Herne shoved me aside and slid out from behind me. He released me so abruptly that I stumbled and fell to the ground. My palms landed on sharp rock shards and the stinging pain let me know they were cut.

I opened my eyes.

The dust cloud settled, making it possible to see. As I pushed up to my feet, I surveyed the situation.

The Herne bolted for the cave's exit with no concern for his fellow miners or anyone else.

The miner who'd thrown the dynamite had disappeared under a pile of broken stalactites. I debated going over to help him, but I knew it was pointless. Besides, the sound of alarmed women's voices reached me.

The singing had stopped with the explosion, and the Ladies of the Lake had scattered. They were gathering themselves and standing up—all but one. They moved in faltering steps toward a Lady who remained still, lying half in and half out of the river water. Her cowl had fallen back to reveal long auburn hair—Rhiannon.

Despite what I would have expected, the rumbling in the rock hadn't abated. If anything, it was gaining strength. Stalactites were breaking loose, and the ground was shaking enough to make walking difficult.

It was another earthquake. I could not believe the horrific timing.

I advanced toward Rhiannon, intent on helping her. Blood stained her robe. The stone beneath me shifted, and I wobbled forward as if I were drunk.

One of the biggest stalactites broke free and landed in the river, sending a splash of water up that soaked me and made the rock slippery. I fell onto my bottom, sputtering. I tried to stand but slipped again. I resigned myself to crawling toward Rhiannon.

A fleeing miner grabbed me, more to steady himself than to capture me. I latched onto him for the same reason and got to my feet. We wobbled there together, trying not to fall. He seemed about my age. Weather-worn and rough like a biker but soft like a new granddad, he probably told dad jokes.

Someone shouted, "Kitty! Dodge!"

My heart skipped a beat. Dodge? Dodge what? Dodge where? Confusion made me slow. Too slow.

I slipped and fell onto my back. My hands tangled in the miner's clothes, and he came with me. From my prone position, I spotted a crack forming at the base of a massive stalactite. It was coming down—right on top of me—of me and the miner.

I froze.

The miner saw it too. He twitched, on the verge of running, but it was too late.

Out of the blue, a shadowy blob flew at my head and hit me in the face. Pain stung my neck, chest, and scalp. Something had latched onto me. Something furry. Something with claws.

I screamed and got a mouthful of fur.

The ground fell away, and my stomach lurched.

What happened next left me confused and frightened. The creature on my face became heavy, hairless, and much bigger. It weighed me down. Was it the stalactite? Was I being crushed? Was it going to suffocate me?

Everything changed. A profound silence surrounded me. Unnatural. It was so quiet, my ears were ringing.

I thought I'd died.

Then, the weight on me lifted. I sucked in a deep breath and stayed on my back, afraid to move, my hand still clutching the miner's shirt—and a few chest hairs as well. I unclenched my eyelids.

I was in a vast, empty space—not white so much as colorless.

And there, sitting beside me, was a naked man.

He said, "Meow."

"Holy Moses!" I cried in surprise and fright. I pushed up and crab-walked away from him.

He was a man but not a man. His head was a mix of man and cat, fuzzy upright ears and a strong masculine jaw. Big, golden eyes stared back at me. "It's okay, Kitty. You're safe now."

My heart raced, and my stomach did flip-flops. Wooziness made me sway and blink rapidly. I swallowed and took a few conscious breaths to keep from puking.

I struggled to sort out what was happening.

"Are you God?" I asked.

"A god." His eyes sparked. "Or more like your guardian angel."

"What? Am I dead?"

"Nearly, but no. I saved you. You're very much alive and safe now." The man sat cross-legged, not the least bit modest about his nudity.

I moved my gaze to his face—too late.

The man just looked calmly at me.

I cleared my throat and managed to say one word, "You're..."

"Magnificent," the cat-man finished for me. "I know."

I was so overwhelmed, I couldn't speak. I took inventory of myself. When I put my fingers to the stinging spots on my chest, they came away with blood on them. I was bruised in places where rocks had struck me, and the scrapes on my palms had stopped bleeding but needed cleaned. Dirt and dust covered my clothes, hair, and skin, but I was not badly injured. My heart slowed, and the nausea eased.

I examined my environment, which was an exercise in frustration. There wasn't anything to see. It was a vast landscape of nothing.

The only other things in it, besides me, were the naked man and the miner, who was throwing up.

"Where are we?" I asked.

"The Interstice. It's the space between realms. Or, to put it in terms you will understand, the secret hallway behind the mall stores."

"You brought us here?"

"Yes. I saved you from certain doom. You're welcome."

"The stalactite."

"Yes."

"And the others?"

"They're not my concern. *You* are my concern."

"Why?"

The man shrugged with cat-like nonchalance. "Just cuz."

I nodded, though I had no idea what that meant.

The miner created a sudden commotion. He stood like a

janky automaton, his body shaking and unsteady. He dug in his jacket packet, appearing to catch his hand in it. Once he freed it, he pointed his gun at the cat-man. He stabbed the gun in that direction a few times.

The cat-man's mouth flattened, as did his ears. Otherwise, he didn't move.

Until he found his words, the miner's jaw moved silently. Finally, he blurted, "What'd you do to me? Where are we?"

"I saved your life. You're in the Interstice. Calm down."

The miner turned the gun on me. "Take me back, or I'll shoot her!"

◆ ◆ ◆

CHAPTER 39

DIANA *gets a big haul.*

A thunderous BOOM sounded deep in the cave system. A cloud of dust rolled out and engulfed us.

Eagle put his arm out in front of me, like Mom used to do in the car whenever she had to brake hard. It halted me in my tracks.

"What was that?" I barely got the words out. My breath caught.

"Explosion." Eagle grabbed my hand. "We need to get out of here."

Even after the boom, the thunder kept going. It reminded me of a STOMP show. The ground started trembling. Crackles and pops punctuated the drumroll. The mountain was coming apart.

"Mom!" I shouted and pulled away before Eagle could stop me.

A stream of people were running out of the cave covered in

a layer of dust. Men. Women. Cops. Not cops.

"Kitty Kats?" I asked them. "Did you see Kitty Kats? Is Kitty Kats in there?"

They all brushed me off in their hurry to escape.

Eagle wrapped a giant hand around my bicep. "Stop."

Panic rose like bile in my gorge, burning and urgent. "Mom's in there!" I pried at Eagle's fingers.

"Wait." Eagle wasn't straining at all. He was surveying the runners, and when a particular miner came toward us, he let me go, curled his hand into a fist, and punched the guy right in the face. No one was more surprised than I.

The man stumbled back but managed not to fall. It was the head miner, the one who had shot at us, the one who had deflowered me in high school—Hunter Herne. He stood up straight, and his whole body tensed. He sneered, eyes squinted and full of anger. Then he launched himself at Eagle.

Eagle released me in order to defend himself.

I saw my opportunity and bolted. My mom was in there somewhere, maybe hurt, maybe worse.

I didn't get far. An aftershock—a nasty one—shook the ground under my feet, and a crevice opened in the floor ahead. It split down the cave, coming toward me.

"Eagle!" I shouted, struggling to stay upright.

The crack shifted to one side and went up the wall.

Someone ran straight toward it from the other side.

I shouted, "Stop! Stop! Stop!"

Despite my warning, the panicked miner didn't even pause. He stepped right off the edge and disappeared with a scream into the crevice. His voice decreased in volume until it just stopped.

I didn't have time to react.

A loud thud sounded behind me, Eagle hitting Herne or Herne hitting Eagle; I didn't know which. I didn't care which, until a heavy male body slammed into my shoulder and spun me around. The unidentified body headed straight for the widening crack.

Another wave of adrenaline rushed into my veins. It happened so fast. I couldn't comprehend it. I held my breath.

The body hit the ground and slid right over the edge of the crack. It was big enough for him to fall into, and gods knew how deep. He couldn't halt his own momentum. He was a goner.

My brain finally registered that it wasn't Eagle. It was Hunter Herne, and I felt an all-too-brief flash of relief.

Then, another body hit my other shoulder, spinning me in the other direction. Eagle launched himself at Herne, landed on his stomach, and just managed to latch onto Herne's wrist.

Herne's bulk started dragging Eagle over the lip.

"Oh my god!" I lurched forward and grabbed Eagle by his waistband. "Let him go!" I dropped my weight into my booty and pulled. "He's not worth it!" The soles of my shoes slid in the dust and gravel.

Eagle strained to pull Herne up, inch by inch. I like to think I helped, though all I may have done was expose half of Eagle's butt. Sorry. Not sorry.

A deputy showed up and helped. That turned the tables. Together, we hauled Herne onto solid ground.

I sat there, panting.

◆ ◆ ◆

CHAPTER 40

MUSE *steps in it.*

The dirty man pointed his gun at Kitty. His hand shook. I didn't trust the gun not to go off. Who knew what a bullet would do under the influence of the Interstice's strange physics? I had to defuse the situation.

"Typical commoner," I mused, pulling his attention to me. "Your species has the unexplainable need to kill anything you don't comprehend. Neanderthal." It worked, to a degree.

The miner pointed the gun at me, but he grew even more frantic. He was spitting mad and his words came out in sputters. I didn't understand a word he said, but I got the gist.

I gave in. I approached him as one would a wounded tomcat.

He shook the weapon and shouted, "Stop!"

I stopped.

"Look," I said. "I need to touch you, or I can't 'chute you home."

Wild-eyed and red-faced—like a baboon butt—the miner took a minute to consider that. He was just as likely to shoot us as he was to let me touch him.

"Heeeeey." Kitty dropped into her soothing-a-feral-cat voice. "It's okay. We're okay. You're safe." She held out her hands, palms up. "What's your name, honey?"

"Larry Doill."

"All right, Mr. Doill. Don't worry. You want to go home, right?"

"Yeah," said Doill. "Now." His stress returned. "Now! I want to go now! Or I swear, I'll kill ya both."

Kitty and I both raised our hands up in surrender.

Help arrived. Old Tom emerged from the fog that wasn't fog and sneaked up on the miner from behind. I felt a wave of relief.

The miner had no clue that Tom was there.

"Okay, dude," I said. "Just relax. No one's going to hurt you."

Old Tom slid right up behind the miner. He palmed the man's skull. The miner cringed, but before he could react, Old Tom shoved the miner's head forward with force. The miner fell and disappeared through a hole in the veil. Just like that. The pop was audible, and then he was gone.

Kitty gasped. I was proud of her. Despite everything, she was holding up like a champion.

I smiled at Tom. "You send him back to the cave?"

When Tom nodded, Kitty gasped again. "That's a death sentence!"

"Hm." Old Tom evaluated Kitty through squinted eyes. "Maybe. He's got about a five percent chance of getting out of there alive." He turned to me. "Besides, he was two seconds away from blowing your head off, sire. Couldn't have that."

"Thanks, Tom."

"You're welcome, sire."

Quietly, Kitty asked, "What kin are you?"

I gestured to Tom because that was exactly the kind of question he loved answering.

Tom said with a regal flourish, "Royal Catkin, madam. From the Place Where Whiskers Grow Long and Strong. Also known as the Whiskers Kingdom. We are, however, in exile. Ousted by a criminal contingency."

"Oh," Kitty said, fluttering her eyelids. She opened her mouth to say more but then closed it.

Tom's ears flicked. "We should—"

Kitty interrupted him. "Why did you save me?"

With another regal flourish, Tom gestured to me.

I said, "Because, Kitty, you are a valued member of my court."

"Your court?"

"If I may, sire?" Old Tom gave a bow. "Madam, allow me to introduce you to the King of the Whiskers Kingdom, his Royal Majesty, King Muse."

I watched Kitty's expression go from curious to confused to shocked.

"Muse?"

I nodded with a most regal demeanor.

"My cat? Muse?"

Amusement bubbled up inside me.

Old Tom said, "Our enemies hexed us. We can't be anything but feline in Reality. Here in the Interstice, you see our true selves."

I smiled. "You're welcome."

Kitty blinked at me. "I guessed there was something special about you."

"Yes. You did." I shared a long stare with Kitty, letting her take in the full extent of my specialness. I knew it was almost more than she could bear.

Old Tom broke the spell. "Sire, we should return her to Reality. Who knows what the spark here is doing to her."

"Of course, Tom. Well advised."

Once our eye contact was broken, Kitty swayed in place. "Do I have to go to the cave, too?"

"No, Kitty. I'll take you back to Faffy and Smaug."

"Faffy and..."

I performed a sneak attack, wrapping my humanoid hand around her arm. Before she could react, I 'chuted us away. The ground fell out from under us, and the world became a whirlpool of colors bleeding into the white. We landed inside the Fishgiven livingroom, and Kitty promptly puked. No hairball, sadly.

I stalked into the kitchen to see what was in the food bowls.

CHAPTER 41

DIANA *leads the perp walk.*

The earthquake was over. My mouth tasted like dirt, and grit made my eyes water, but Eagle and I were alive.

In the quiet that ensued, the distant sound of singing reached me. Women's voices, from somewhere out of sight in the cave, rose in harmony. They sang a gentle, beautiful song. It made me feel as if the world would survive after all.

That didn't last long. Mom was in there. "Eagle," I said, my voice shaking. "We need to find my Mom."

Eagle came over to me, leaving the deputy on his own to handcuff Herne the Miner.

"We will." His heavy hand came to rest on my shoulder. "We're not getting past that crack though."

"What about the other entrance?" The thought of going through that tunnel made my stomach rebel.

"No." Eagle shook his head. "God knows what damage the earthquakes have done to it. We just need some tools. Something to bridge that gap. We'll figure it out. Your mom's tough. And she's not alone."

The healing lullaby continued to echo off the rock.

Eagle offered me a hand. "Let's get out of here before there's another aftershock."

I put my small hand in his much larger one, feeling like a child who had lost her mommy at the department store.

The detective perp-walked Herne out. Eagle and I took the lead. At the entrance to the cave, we found an angry anthill of police, rescue, and fire. Mom's Eli was there, shouting orders. Medical personnel were treating the injured, wounds from either gunshots or falling rocks. Metal gurneys rattled across rough terrain.

Herne, with his deputy at his elbow, joined the procession

toward the parking area.

My phone rang.

Surprised, I pulled it from my pocket. It had, somehow, re-mained undamaged.

It was my mom.

"Mom!" I moved to one side to get away from the cacophony of voices. "Mom, where are you? Are you okay?"

"Hi, honey. Where are *you?*" She sounded fine.

"Mom, what's happening? I heard they'd taken you hostage. Did you escape?"

"Oh, sweetie. You know me. I'm fine. I'm at Martha's."

"At Martha's!" My knees melted with relief, and I had to sit down on a big rock. "Jeez, Mom. I was so worried."

"I'm sorry, Di. I've been calling and texting. You didn't an-swer."

"I was in the cave. No reception." My hands were shaking. "So, you *weren't* in the cave?"

"Oh, no. I was definitely there. You didn't go in, did you? I hope you let the police handle things. Is Eagle there with you?"

I took a breath before answering. "Yes, he's here. We're fine."

"Bring him over, and I'll make sloppy joes. We can talk about what happened."

"Can I stay there with you tonight?"

"Of course, honey. I'd like that."

An alarm of shouts went up, and the deputies took off run-ning toward the parking area.

"Mom, I have to go. We'll be there soon."

"Drive safe!"

Eagle had already started down the trail, and I ran to catch up with him.

"What's going on?"

"Dunno. Stay close to me."

We approached the clearing with caution, but the excite-ment was dissipating. The Herne had escaped and stolen a sher-iff's vehicle. They'd gone after him, of course, and that was all someone else's problem.

"Mom's at Martha's. She's cooking. You hungry?"

"Starving."

I slapped Eagle on the back. "Let's make like balls and bounce."

Eagle snorted a laugh.

I realized the double entendre, but I didn't apologize. I just grinned.

◆ ◆ ◆

CHAPTER 42

KITTY *gets a hug.*

Peace and quiet were returning. The night of the quake, I'd relayed to Diana and Eagle what had happened— mostly. It wasn't my place to out Muse, so I told them the Ladies of the Lake had rescued me. A tiny white lie couldn't hurt.

I slept like a cat that night, my tummy filled with comfort food and my mind eased, knowing Diana was safe and snoring in the bed beside me. I watched her sleep for a while, snuggled up to her dog. My mother's heart swelled with love and gratitude.

The next morning, I made us breakfast, then Di decided to take another shower.

"I've still got dirt in my ears and hair," she complained, scratching her scalp.

"Maybe do a more thorough job this time?"

"I was so tired last night, I could barely see. Why are all Martha's clothes baby colors?"

I closed my eyes and took a breath. "You can't wear the filthy ones you showed up in. Just put anything on. You can grab more from home later. You look pretty in pink. No one will care."

"I'll care!"

I left her to her drama. "C'mon, Muse."

I grabbed my coffee, and Muse and I went outside on the back patio. We sat in companionable silence, listening to the birds and watching the sunlight sparkle on the water. It would have been an idyllic view, except for the whirlpool. The sinkhole had continued overnight, slowly draining the lake. The trees at its edge were tipping and sliding in.

The spire reminded me of bone exposed by torn flesh. In the open, it lost its mystique.

The earthquake had forever changed Talyllyn and Wyrdwood. Local news couldn't stop talking about it.

A contingent of folks stood on the far shore. Even at that distance, I recognized the mayor among them by her bright red shock of hair. I assumed they were working spells to conceal the spire. Normals wouldn't understand. They'd send looky-loos like archeologists and alien-hunters. What a P.R. nightmare.

As I contemplated everything that had happened, something moved in the water at the lakeshore. It looked like a fancy goldfish, swimming casually, its fins spread out and catching the dappled sunlight.

The fins became Rhiannon's hair, and she walked out of the water. Merlynn came with her.

Both naked and unashamed, they held hands and climbed the stairs toward me. Water drained off them, leaving a trail in their wake. An aura of sadness surrounded them. They moved slowly, and their eyes remained downcast.

Muse retreated to the far corner of the patio. He didn't seem to trust the Ladies of the Lake, but he didn't hiss or growl.

Rhiannon said nothing until she was in front of me. I stayed seated so I wouldn't tower over them on the upper stair.

"We have come to see you, Kitty Kats." Rhiannon's tone was grave.

"What a pleasant surprise. Are you feeling better?"

Rhiannon tipped her head. "My sisters took care of me. I am well. And you? I saw...you with the stag-man."

"He didn't hurt me."

Rhiannon regarded her daughter. "We are leaving Talyllyn,"

she said. "Merlynn wants to say goodbye to you."

"Oh, that's so nice. Thank you. I'm sorry you have to leave, honey."

Merlynn glanced up at me with sad eyes.

I asked, "Where will you go?"

"We must withdraw fully into our own realm. Reality has grown too dangerous for us."

"So, the sinkhole is going to drain the lake completely?"

"I think not. The caverns below will fill with water, and then it will level out again. But it can never be as sacred as it was."

Many more questions bubbled to the surface of my mind. How will you make babies? Will you ever return? What will happen to your boys? But I didn't ask them. I didn't want to be *that* woman. Besides, the decision had obviously been a difficult one, and neither of my new friends was happy about it. I saw no need to pour salt on their wounds.

Sometimes, you're powerless to make things right. At those times, you can only try not to make things worse.

"I'm sorry," I said. "Truly, my dears. Truly sorry."

Rhiannon put an arm around Merlynn. "You are kind, Kitty Kats. Thank you for all you have done for Merlynn."

"I only fed her cookies and a bit of love."

"You did more than that."

I sat up and held my arms out to Merlynn. "Can I have a hug? Do your people hug?"

The child had to check with her mother first.

Rhiannon gave her a loving look. "We hug. Don't we, Mer? Go ahead."

Merlynn walked to me and wrapped her arms around my neck. I hugged her warm skinny body to me. She smelled of lake water, blue-green and summery.

"Don't worry," I told her. "Everything's going to be okay. You'll see."

With a quick peck to my cheek, she released me.

Her mother said, "Stay close to King Muse. He will keep you safe in the troubled times to come. He is more than he appears."

"So I'm learning." I chuckled with surprise. "I will."

An easy silence fell upon us for a few seconds while I debated whether to ask one final question. It popped out on its own. "What about the giant?"

"It sleeps. For now. But there are those who want it to awaken. If that happens, you must take your loved ones and flee to another realm. It *will* destroy this world."

"Okay." There was nothing more to say. I, however, had plenty of thinking—and planning—to do.

As the Ladies of the Lake turned to go, Merlynn and I exchanged waves.

I sipped my coffee and watched them enter the lake. A sense of loss struck me. The world—Reality—was becoming less magickal. It hurt my heart.

◆ ◆ ◆

CHAPTER 43

DIANA *spills the tea.*

The events of the previous day had unsettled me, and I planned to stick close to Mom. I was not, however, willing to wear Martha's pastel old-lady clothes for long. The ones I'd arrived in were dusty and torn from our adventure in the cave.

When Eagle called, he caught me up on all the news and offered to drive me home. I jumped at the chance to save a few bucks on an e-taxi.

I had a few minutes to kill, so I joined Mom on the patio. "Eagle's coming to get me," I told her. "Do you mind if I leave Mimi here with you? I'll be back before she needs walkies again."

I shooed the cat out of the chair.

The jerk hissed at me, but he moved. I took his seat and watched as he sat and cleaned himself with far too much dignity. Something told me he was congratulating himself for giving his seat to a lady. Such a gentleman. Not.

Mom asked, "Tell me again how you met Eagle?"

"He came to me. Needed someone with a spark. He's human."

"Superhuman, more like."

"Can't disagree." I studied Mom more closely. In the light of day, I could see she had a few bruises—on her chin, her wrist, and her forehead—but otherwise, she appeared unharmed. "Hunter Herne is in custody. He got away from the deputies, but the mayor's people caught him. Idiot."

"Eagle filled you in?"

"Yeah."

"How many were killed?"

"Two miners. No deputies. Most everyone had injuries, though. Between the flying bullets and the falling rocks..."

Mom leaned forward. "What about Larry Doill?"

"Larry Doill?" I knew that name far too well. He was Brenda Doill's father—my nemesis's father. Whenever we were in the principal's office for fighting, he'd always taken her side. "What was he doing there?"

"Mining. He was one of them. Why? You know him?"

"I know his daughter. She...works with me. I hope he wasn't the one who blew himself up."

"No." My mom didn't seem quite herself. She was more quiet than usual. Low energy. "Did you hear whether he got out alive?"

"All I know is that two miners died. Eagle might know. I'll ask him for you." When Mom sat back and said nothing, I continued. "The mayor interrogated Hunter Herne last night. She put him under one of those truth spells she loves so much. Apparently, he was the one sneaking around here."

"Did he confess to killing Harold?"

"No. The opposite, actually. He swore he didn't. He killed others, but Harold wasn't one of them."

"Oh, that's too bad."

"That he didn't kill Uncle Harold?"

"It would tie all this up with a neat bow." Mom's expression turned sad and nostalgic.

"Mom, it was an accident."

"Sure," Mom said. "Bad luck."

I leaned forward and put my hand on her forearm. "What's the matter, Mom? You can talk to me, you know?"

Eagle, with his usual impeccable timing, came around the side of the house.

"Mornin'," he said. "You ready to go?"

I hesitated then got to my feet. "Yeah. Let me grab my backpack."

As I went into the house, I heard Mom say, "Eagle?"

"Yes, ma'am."

"When is murder not a murder?"

I paused, intrigued enough to eavesdrop.

Eagle let out a puff of air, thinking. "Not sure I can answer that. I reckon there are many situations that blur the line. The killer's intent matters, I guess."

"In the eyes of the law?"

Eagle took too long to reply. The cats nosed around the door, so I had to pull it shut. If Eagle answered, I didn't hear it. By the time I got back to the patio, they were both silent and staring at the lake.

◆ ◆ ◆

Wily like a coyote.
Crazy like a fox.
Snarky like a cat.
—T-shirt

◆

CHAPTER 44

MUSE *confronts Scratch.*

When is murder not a murder? It was the most ridiculous question of a most ridiculous day. When Kitty asked it, Diana's ape friend thought so hard he built up static electricity.

"I think," he finally said, "the only time murder isn't murder is when it isn't murder."

I stopped breathing, awed. Never had I heard anything so completely, so quintessentially moronic. *Murder isn't murder if it isn't murder.* And the monkey keeps slamming the typewriter keys.

I'd had enough. Diana usurping my chair had stung. Then, the caveman had arrived to distract me. I didn't have time for mundanities. I had truly important business to ponder—specifically Scratch. He was still out there somewhere, and I needed to go on the offensive. My guts had healed up enough that I felt ready for a fight—if he brought one on.

Thanks to Old Tom's gift, moving in and out of the Interstice was becoming easy. I willed myself to the front porch of Kitty's house—the front porch of *my* house. With each passing day, I grew more possessive of her. More so since she'd met my true self. And she'd heard my voice in her head. When the rocks were falling, I ordered her to dodge. She heard me. She may not realize it, but she did. That was monumental and one more reason why I had no intention of leaving her—unless, of course, Scratch *murdered* me. Real murder is murder, especially when it's murder. And especially when they're murdering your beloved mate.

I heaved a great sigh.

It took me a few seconds to find Scratch. He was lying in the grass at the foot of the mailbox, watching me. As soon as my eyes met his, he got to his feet. I saw the stiffness in his joints and the wobble in his balance. To his credit, he gathered himself and puffed to make himself seem bigger.

Time to toss the dog a bone—as they say.

I walked toward Scratch, relaxed, gaze averted. There was nothing submissive in my demeanor but nothing aggressive either.

Scratch eyed me with suspicion, but didn't menace me. He was waiting to see what I would do.

I stopped a respectable distance away, non-threatening, and lay down in the grass. If necessary, I could leap forward in an instant. Scratch knew that.

"You killed my mate," I said, observing Scratch with half an eye.

"I did. Do you want to make me pay for that?"

"I do."

"I was following orders."

"I know."

"It was hundreds of years ago."

"It was."

"I'm sorry."

I'd imagined confronting him a billion times, fantasized about killing him in a thousand painful ways, but never had I expected to hear those words.

A breeze played across the tips of the grass and made the leaves rustle in the trees. The sunshine blanketed my back with melancholy warmth.

What can I say? I was feeling merciful. The truth was, I rarely thought of my love anymore. In the hundreds of years since her death, I'd had many others. And so, even face-to-face with my betrayer, I couldn't muster enough of a pluck to take my revenge.

"You're lucky," I said.

"Lucky?"

"I'm older now. Wiser. And I have more important things to do besides tear your throat out."

"Oh."

I sat up and placed my front paws together with royal prissiness. "Why did you come here?"

"Because I owe you."

"Tell me more."

"Our kingdom. Your kingdom. It's…"

I put all my power into a single command. "Spit it out."

"It's gone, sire."

I wasn't sure what bothered me more. The fact that he'd said my realm was "gone," or the fact that he'd dared to call me "sire" after everything he'd done to oust me. I gritted my teeth and focused on the former.

"What are you talking about?"

"The Place Where Whiskers Grow Long and Strong is no more."

I pounced. My jaws went for Scratch's neck.

He rolled over, exposing his belly. "Please, sire!"

I stopped before breaking his skin. I didn't clamp down, but he knew I would, could, and maybe even should. I commanded, "Tell me!"

Scratch's front paw twitched, and I smelled his pee. "Magick was dying, sire. The leaders tried to save it with a pandaurus orb from another realm. It contained more magick than we'd ever known. When they opened it, just a crack, nothing but chaos came out. We had war after war for a hundred years until nothing remained. Our people starved or were killed in battle. At the end, someone shattered the orb, and the chaos tore our world apart. I barely got out in time."

I sat back, in shock. "You're lying."

Scratch stayed in a submissive position. "No, sire. I wish I were."

My mind refused to accept what I was hearing. "Show me. Take me there."

"There's no place to take you to. That's what I'm trying to tell you. It disintegrated. It melted back into the cosmos."

I looked at Scratch—really looked at him. His pupils had exploded. He was scared of more than just me.

"Why didn't you tell me sooner?"

"You attacked me, sire." He bowed his head. " Rightly so. But I had to defend myself."

"Why didn't you tell me when it was happening? I might have…"

Scratch whispered, "I never thought it would go so far. None of us did."

I had no idea whether I could trust anything he said. I'd fallen for his treachery once before and lived to regret it.

"Why come to me now?"

He cracked open his scraggly mouth, revealing a snaggletooth and blackened lips.

I waited.

After a few seconds, he said, "I have nowhere else to go, sire. You and I may be the last of our kin."

Anguish washed over me, but I couldn't let him see it. Every muscle in my body tensed so I could speak without feeling. "Go now. Come back tomorrow. I need time…"

"Yes, sire. Thank you, sire."

I watched him go until he was out of sight beyond the neighbor's garage. Only then did I stand. I lifted my face and yowled at the sun. How dare it shine so sweetly when my beloved Place Where Whiskers Grow Long and Strong was destroyed!

I needed Kitty and her comforting hands. With my last reserves of energy, I zoomed around the side of the house and into the bushes. There, hidden from view, I 'chuted through the Interstice and back to the lake house, where I found Kitty's loving care.

◆ ◆ ◆

CHAPTER 45

KITTY *informs Martha.*

Muse suddenly appeared on the patio. As cats do. More surprisingly, he jumped onto my lap and rubbed his face against my hand.

I hadn't moved from my seat except to retrieve a second cup of coffee and a blueberry muffin from the kitchen.

Petting Muse took on a new dimension that made me uneasy. I stuck to scritching his head and back, and I avoided his tummy. I kept seeing his naked man-form in my mind. He was so loving and insistent, though.

"You okay, bud?" I asked.

He rolled onto his side across my thighs.

"It's been a rough few days, hasn't it? For me too. It's all right. We'll get through it together, okay? You and me, honey."

The patio door slid open.

"Who are you talking to?"

I looked around, but I'd already recognized the voice. "The cat, of course. You're back. How was England?"

"Dreary." Martha eased her way to the second chair and sat. She appeared even older and weaker than she had before she left. "I saw my babies. They look healthy and happy. Thank you, Kitty, for taking such great care of them."

"I'm sorry the house is such a mess. We had a big earthquake last night, and I—"

"Oh my goodness! Is that a sinkhole?" Martha sat forward, squinting to see better.

"Yes."

"We haven't had one of those here since I was a girl."

I no longer recognized my friend, and I realized I was the one who had changed, not her. I was seeing her from a different perspective.

"Martha. Did you kill Harold?"

She was taken aback, but only because I'd figured it out. "Let it go, Kitty. Harold's luck ran out. Plain and simple."

There it was, as direct a confession as I could want. "You found out about his other wife," I said. "About his children."

Martha relaxed back in her chair again. "We were married for over thirty years, Kitty. Thirty years of lies. Oh, and he was skilled at it, too. I never once suspected. Not once."

"I'm sorry." I was no stranger to the duplicity of men—although my husband had never cheated on me, that I knew.

"What was worse was that everything changed when he broke that covenant. His health went downhill. Our finances tanked. And his so-called business partners came for their takes. Harold was like that sinkhole, sucking all that was good down with him. Our beautiful life. Me."

She paused, lost in thought. Her voice grew hard. "You know what he asked me to do? He asked me to go to her and apologize for him. He wanted *me* to grovel at her feet and beg her to take him back because he was too crippled to do it himself."

I had no reply, so I waited for her to continue.

"Faffy, Smaug, and I are leaving Wyrdwood, Kitty. Harold bequeathed me enough that I can go away and live my remaining years in peace. Somewhere pretty, with a rose garden, and no lakes."

I was in shock. What a horrible ending to our friendship. No fireworks. No dancing. Just death and betrayal. I was glad Bob wasn't there to witness it. It would've broken his heart.

I felt the frown harden on my face and licked my lips to try to loosen it.

Martha pulled her purse onto her lap and opened it. "I have something I want to give you, my dear." She took out a small jewelry box and handed it to me.

I tried to wave it away, but she insisted. "Please. It would mean so much to me if you had it."

Martha's expression was resigned. She knew that she'd lost my friendship. Maybe she even feared I'd turn her in. I hadn't decided whether or not I would. A part of me hated Harold for how he'd wounded her.

The jewelry box held a gold pendant. Pure gold. The pendant was flat and oval, like a cartouche. It was the length of my thumb and had a small hole at one end for a chain or cord. The jeweler had stamped a symbol into it, a fish curved as if leaping from the water.

"It's a talisman bar," Martha explained. "It will keep you safe. The gold is from the mountain."

I closed the box and tried to hand it back. "I can't take this, Martha. It must be worth a fortune."

Martha pushed it toward me. "Please. I want you to know how grateful I am for your friendship. We had so many happy years, didn't we?"

"I have a ton of good memories in this house. Will you sell it?"

"Perhaps. Would you like to have it? I have more money than I know what to do with—thanks to Harold."

My eyebrows flew up, but I wasn't even tempted to say yes, not for one second. "No, thank you. *Too many* memories. Now that Bob's gone, they weigh on me."

Martha nodded as if she understood.

Bob leans against the railing, one hand tucked in his trouser pocket. He's smoking a cigarette and gazing out at the lake. His hair is brown, not gray. His belly is flat, no pooch. His shoes are polished, the crease in his pants sharp, and his shirt sky-blue and starched.

He's gorgeous.

The sun is setting in the distance, painting the sky with watercolor pastels that reflect on the water. As if aware that I'm watching him, he turns to meet my gaze. A smile plays on his lips, and his adoration shows in the way his eyes crinkle at the edges. I am overcome with love.

I stood up, much to Muse's dismay. "I should go. You take care of yourself, Martha. And let Faffy and Smaug comfort you."

"All I can hope for now is comfort." Martha started to get up, but I put my hand out to stop her.

"Stay here and relax. I'll get my things and call an e-taxi."

Martha lowered herself back into the chair with a relieved sigh. "All right, Kitty. Yell if you need me."

"I will."

Martha's words returned to haunt me: "This is how our beautiful life ends."

I went into the house. Muse scooted in too. A sombre silence had settled upon the lake house. It didn't take me long to pack and put Mimi in her carrier.

I stopped to kiss Faffy and Smaug on their heads, but I skipped saying goodbye to Martha. I knew it would be the last time, and I couldn't face that. I left the keys on the counter.

Muse, bless his big heart, stayed by my side the whole ride home.

◆ ◆ ◆

CHAPTER 46

DIANA *and Kitty recline.*

Not long after the earthquake, Martha returned, and Mom came home. She and I started having movie nights. She sat in her recliner, and I in Dad's. Mom used to say, "There's nothing sadder than a barren recliner." It was what gave me the idea to do our first movie night. A love of movies was the one thing Mom and I had in common. Plus, it was fun.

We ate popcorn and watched chick flicks or geeky fantasy films. We'd put our feet up, snuggle under soft throws, and hold our pets in our laps—Mimi in mine, and Muse in hers. It was the closest to Heaven I ever expected to get.

We were settling in to watch the latest Sandra Bullock. Mom

handed me a glass of soda and said, "I want to scatter your father's ashes at Talyllyn Lake."

She couldn't have shocked me more. I glanced over at the urn on the bureau. "Okay. Why?"

Mom sat in her recliner. "It just makes sense. We had many wonderful summers out there. So much happiness."

"What about the sinkhole?"

"Well, they say the chamber below the lake must be full now. The levels aren't dropping any longer. It's stabilized."

"Okay."

Mom held her own soda glass in both hands, and I was struck by how delicate her fingers were. I knew them to be strong, but I'd never noticed their grace until just then. She said, "I want to make it a kind of ceremony. Putting the past with the past, so we can move forward unencumbered. The past is..."

I finished for her. "...unreliable."

"Exactly," she said. "Will you come with me?"

"Of course."

"And are you okay with us making it a ceremony. A good-bye?"

Tears tickled my nose. "If that's what you want, I'm with you."

"Thank you. I'll let you know when I'm ready." Mom got up, leaned over me, and hugged me. "I love you, honey," she said. The tears on our cheeks mingled.

Mom returned to her chair and popped her footrest up. I started the movie. As the opening sequence played, she said, "By the way, I'm going back to that warlock. I need to ditch this curse."

I turned my head slowly, deliberately, to stare at her. "Mom," I said. "You are *not* cursed."

"Shhh," she said and pointed at the TV.

Muse jumped up onto her legs and tucked himself between her knees. He really was cute—for a cat.

◆ ◆ ◆

POSTMORTEM

MAYOR VIOLET BAGLEY *closes the case.*

ase resolved. We rounded up all but one of the surviving miners. They face punishment for assault with a deadly weapon, public endangerment, resisting arrest, and more. We acquired Bareface confessions from all of them.

I incarcerated Hunter Herne IV in the Wyrdwood dungeons. He will serve a year and a day.

The miner—Terrance Flunt—who confessed to murdering Sallipose, a Lady of the Lake, was mercifully executed.

Unfortunately, the location of the missing miner remains a mystery even to his coworkers. He used an alias—Jock, no last name—while working the mine. He disguised his physical features under a magickal veil. We have an image of his public face, but he has undoubtedly changed his appearance.

Meanwhile, I deposed the primary witnesses (with informed consent) under the influence of a Bareface spell, as required by Wyrdwood law. Kitty Kats revealed the name of the missing miner: Larry Doill. We found neither him nor his body in the cave. I filed a BOLO order with local law enforcement.

Her investigation into Harold Fishgiven bore impressive fruit. I know—though she doesn't know that I know—Martha Fishgiven brought about her husband's death. Mrs. Kats did her best to hide this information from me, despite the Bareface charm. I admire her loyalty.

Although Normal law would see it differently, I've come to the same conclusion regarding Martha's punishment as Mrs. Kats. Martha Fishgiven will not be charged. Her husband was more than just a bigamist. He was the head of the illegal mining operation and responsible for disturbing the giant. This resulted in lives lost. It also caused the exodus of the Ladies of the Lake from Wyrdwood—a deeply regrettable loss. And it's going to cost the town a small fortune to keep tourists from spotting the spire in Talyllyn Lake.

Harold's punishment would have been the same whether inflicted by his vengeful wife or by me. His crimes were selfish to the point of heinous. Therefore, I see no reason to further darken Martha's waning years.

I also questioned King Muse. I will continue to watch his story unfold with much interest. Learning about his home stratum's destruction shook him. He may begin to act out in unpredictable ways. The messenger from the Whiskers Kingdom—the catkin known as Scratch—accepted a meeting with me. I informed him—in no uncertain terms—of Wyrdwood's laws and the penalties for breaking them. He agreed to behave. Thus, he is welcome to stay.

Lastly, I've approved Diana Kats to work with Eagle Crenshaw and will pay her a small stipend for her time. She's proven useful, and Crenshaw speaks highly of her. Her bravery during the cave collapse saved lives.

[End Incident Report — Fishgiven Illegal Mining Operation, filed by Violet Bagley, Mayor, Wyrdwood, Oregon.]

Thanks for Reading
WW20923

I hope you enjoyed *Catsitter's Curse*. Kitty, Diana, and Muse will be back in their third adventure: *Catsitter's Collar* (2024).

Join our growing community by signing up for the Wyrdwood email list. We'll send instructions for how to connect with other magickal readers just like you. Sign up now at the link below.

If you enjoyed this story, *please* give it a review where you purchased it. It's the kindest gift you can give the authors you love and who love you back (like me!).

READ MORE:
https://www.angelmccoy.com/wyrdwood-home/

Know anyone you think would like this story?

Please let them know about it!

They'll be thankful you did and so will I.

◆ ◆ ◆

From: Angel Leigh McCoy

Wyrdwood is the town I wish I lived in, and its residents are the people I wish were my friends and enemies.

Life can be so sad and terrifying—for us all. Sometimes it's easy to forget what saves us from that. I hope these books remind you that—even in our darkest hours—there is hope, light, love, and laughter.

About me: I'm the spark of creative force behind the darkly fanciful Wyrdwood project and the spooky Dire Multiverse.

I'm an award-winning video game writer who co-developed stories and characters for millions of players (CONTROL, *Guild Wars 2,* and White Wolf's *World of Darkness).*

After two decades in the big city (Seattle), I've settled down in a Gilmore-Girl small town not unlike Wyrdwood. Life is an adventure—every day.

Follow me: https://angelmccoy.com/linktree/
- Facebook: angel.mccoy
- Instagram: angelleighmccoy

Copyright

Catsitter's Curse

Copyright © 2023, Angel Leigh McCoy
Cover copyright © 2023, Angel Leigh McCoy
Catsitter Mysteries series title copyright © 2022, Angel Leigh McCoy
First digital publication: 2023
First print publication: 2023

All rights are reserved. No part of this book may be used or reproduced in any manner without written permission, except in the case of brief quotations embodied in critical articles and reviews. The unauthorized reproduction or distribution of this copyrighted work is illegal.

No part of this book may be scanned, uploaded, or distributed via the Internet or any other means, electronic or print, without the publisher's permission.

This book is a work of fiction. The names, characters, places, and incidents are products of the writer's imagination or have been used fictitiously and are not to be construed as real. Any resemblance to persons living or dead, actual events, locales, or organizations is entirely coincidental.

Published in Macomb, Illinois, United States
by Wily Writers LLC, 2023.

EBook ISBN-13: 978-1-950427-23-9
Print ISBN-13: 978-1-950427-22-2

Read the Wyrdwood Welcome trilogy.

Paperback ◆ Ebook ◆ Audiobook

**Viviane is in love
with a man who remembers
nothing about himself.**

When his past catches up to him, it's stranger and more dangerous than anything Viviane could have imagined. She becomes entangled in a family feud that she's hardly prepared for. Ultimately, she must go to extreme measures to save both him and herself, and in the process, she learns more about herself—and her magickal powers—than she ever wanted to know.

Nothing in Viviane's world is as mundane as she thought it was. Especially not her fiancé. It's a long fall from the moon, and her reality will never be the same.

Contains mature themes.

Don't miss the first Catsitter Mysteries book.

Paperback ◆ Ebook

From Wyrdwood,
the Catsitter Mysteries series, Book #1.

Catsitter Kitty Kats has one problem that's bigger than all her others. She's been targeted by a ruthless arsonist. Can she figure out who it is before it's too late?

This paranormal mystery set in Wyrdwood will keep you guessing right up to the epic ending.

The Wyrdwood Historical Society presents
three free stories:

"Pipsqueak"
"Nurse Magdaleine"
"Charlie Darwin"

Free to download
at AngelMcCoy.com

www.ingramcontent.com/pod-product-compliance
Lightning Source LLC
Chambersburg PA
CBHW030758190726
48285CB00003B/912